FOURFRONT

FOURFRONT

Contemporary stories translated from the Irish

Micheál Ó Conghaile
Pádraic Breathnach
Dara Ó Conaola
Alan Titley

Introduced by
Declan Kiberd

Cló Iar-Chonnachta
Indreabhán
Conamara

First Published 1998
2nd Edition 2001
© Cló Iar-Chonnachta 1998

ISBN 1 902420 01 2

Cover Artwork: Pádraig Reaney
Cover Design: Johan Hofsteenge
Design: CIC

Cló Iar-Chonnachta receives financial assistance from **The Arts Council**

Publisher: Cló Iar-Chonnachta, Indreabhán, Conamara
    Tel: 091-593307   Fax: 091-593362   e-mail: cic@iol.ie
Printing: Clódóirí Lurgan, Indreabhán, Conamara
    Tel: 091-593251/593157

INDEX

Declan Kiberd
Introduction   7

Micheál Ó Conghaile
Death at a Funeral   13
Father   20
Seven Hundred Watches   28
The Man Who Exploded   37

Pádraic Breathnach
A Bucket of Poteen   49
Purple Plums   61
A Fateful Day   65
Precious Moments   72

Dara Ó Conaola
Night Ructions   81
Sorely Pressed   85
Celebration   91
Someone Else   97

Alan Titley
The Judgement   105
The Gobspiel According to John   121
The Last Butterfly   132
Fables   137

Introduction

The short story has flourished as a literary form in those places where a vibrant oral culture has been challenged by the onset of a tradition of written literature. The American Midwest produced Mark Twain, Sherwood Anderson and Ernest Hemingway in direct succession, just as Russia came up with a Chekhov and Normandy with a Maupassant. Many of the finest works by these otherwise disparate authors take for theme that very clash between ancient and modern standards in their peripheral communities, a clash which may indeed have made the very development of the genre possible.

Ireland has produced many great short story writers from George Moore to Mary Lavin, but also, and uncharacteristically, a set of theories with which the form might be interpreted. Two gifted exponents, Sean O'Faolain and Frank O'Connor, wrote treatises on it which are still cited by experts in schools of writing: *The Short Story* and *The Lonely Voice* respectively. Perhaps this was simply a reflection of the intensity with which the genre has been discussed and studied among the broad community. For every decade of the past century, it has been arguably the most popular of all literary forms with Irish writers and, just as important, readers.

Broadsheet newspapers (notably *The Irish Press* and *Sunday Tribune* on a weekly basis, but also *The Irish Times* in summer) have printed stories on an entire page – sometimes to announce a new talent, otherwise to publish a scoop by an established favourite. This tradition goes back a long time, to the days when George Russell published an early story of James Joyce in the *Irish Homestead*. The national radio station has broadcast stories weekly and has energised aspiring writers with well-publicised, much-contested awards. Even the other official genres pay homage to the form: the plays of a Brian Friel or Tom Murphy often can seem like dramatised collections of stories, just as the movies of a Jim Sheridan or a Neil Jordan have that same episodic quality which has led many readers of *Ulysses* to conclude that it is really a sequence of short stories in the drag of an experimental novel.

So popular, even healthily vulgar, has the form become that two decades ago one of the foremost Irish-language novelists of the younger generation protested against the fetishising of the short story as a "quintessentially Irish" form. He called his essay "The Disease of the Irish Short Story" and he urged a moratorium, while writers applied themselves to the more arduous task of constructing good novels. That uncompromising critic, Alan Titley, is none the less represented in this collection by four striking testimonials to the persistence of the shorter form.

In the earlier decades of the twentieth century, the short story was well calibrated to capture the nature of an emergent new society. If the novel chronicled a made society, the story better captured one still in the making: and it did this, as O'Faolain insisted, by concentrating on unconventional individuals who carried in their original way of looking at things the promise of a new dispensation. If the great Anglo-Irish artists like Yeats, Gregory and Synge excelled in poetry and drama, the short story seemed mainly the preserve of the "risen people", the O'Flahertys and the MacMahons, the Os and the Macs. These were authors who in growing up read the classics of English literature but who were also still able to listen to old story-tellers who had honed their skills in oral narrative in the age-old tradition. Of its very nature, the short story as a genre was well suited to registering the upheavals of a society as it shed its ancient traditions. Frank O'Connor has observed that without the concept of a normal society, the novel is impossible: but he has added that the short story is especially appropriate to the place in which constant upheavals have shattered the very idea of community.

This may be a major reason for the persistence of the form in postmodern Ireland, a country which has to undergo in the past century the sort of changes which in other parts of western Europe have been more gradually implemented over, say, three centuries. O'Connor believed that the short story provided a "lonely voice" for members of submerged population groups, for vulnerable minorities faced with the catastrophic onset of modernity and all the possibilities and pitfalls which that implied. There could hardly be a better description of the world inhabited by the dissidents and rebels of Micheál Ó Conghaile's stories, protagonists who find themselves suddenly revealed as "errata" in someone else's master-narrative. Even as the Irish nation-state took on an inexorable form, in the very desire of its leaders to impose a sense of normality after centuries of turbulence it helped to create the conditions for individual dissent and, thus, for new versions of the short story. The only difference was that where once the "submerged population group" might be a flying column of revolutionary gunmen, in later decades it was more likely to be a wounded group of homosexual persons or a lonely bunch of eccentrics.

In fact, Irish speakers and writers in that language now form just one of the many minority groupings clustered within the larger national narrative. Officially esteemed by the state in theory, they have often felt marginalised in daily practice, being treated as at once a national treasure and a practical nuisance. Moreover, within the Irish-speaking movement, creative writers have tended to represent its radical, subversive side rather than its more strait-laced element. Some, like Titley, have voiced their own reservations about the po-face of official Ireland with a linguistic virtuosity that verges on the carnivalesque: proof, if proof were needed, that a loquacious wordplay is not the sole preserve of Irish writers of English, but an intrinsic part of Gaelic tradition, which always prized the phrase-maker and alliterator. Others, such as Pádraic Breathnach, have placed their central focus on isolated individuals whose struggle with inherited authority-structures may tell us more than any sociologist about the destiny of community. And all, like Dara Ó Conaola, have written on the understanding that the short story's real generic affinities are with that other favoured form of Gaelic tradition, the lyric poem. In almost every one of the following stories, there comes a moment of revelation, when the actual surfaces of things take on a wider symbolic meaning, as in a moment of poetry. This is surely the ultimate answer to those who contend that the short story is an "easy" form: for at its best it has the intensity and lyric power of a symbolist poem. Perhaps it was something of that kind which Liam O'Flaherty had in mind when he mischievously suggested that if you could describe a chicken crossing a road, then you were a real writer.

Of necessity, something is lost in a translation to English, a language which an earlier nationalist generation often believed to be utterly alien to the Gaelic mind (whatever that is). But much is also gained: a fairly literal translation recalls for readers that rich, rural English, still vibrant in some places but always in danger of being homogenised by television (which seems to have little space for dialect, for quirkiness, for the individual genius i.e. those very forces which the short story exists to defend).

The language of these versions is often like that of the countrymen and women who impressed the poet Yeats by their capacity to think still in Irish while using English words. (This is the very reverse of the process, painfully obvious to all who have sat in Ireland's classrooms, whereby so many people have to think in English while using Irish words.) And there is a lesson here: that those who translate a tradition, including those who attack it in that very act of translation, may ultimately do more to defend and develop it than those who put the relics of a "folk past" into glass cases for the approval of antiquarians and tourists. Here, on the contrary, is a book which demonstrates that the example of Kafka has been as fully assimilated as that of *Leabhar Sheáin Í Chonaill*. The mingled, gloriously impure nature of our world is well expressed in this most hybrid of literary forms.

Declan Kiberd
Dublin: July 1998

MICHEÁL Ó CONGHAILE

Born in 1962, a native of the Connemara Gaeltacht. One of Ireland's foremost contemporary Irish-language prose writers. Also a publisher. Has written several books, including a social history of Connemara and the Aran Islands: *Conamara agus Árainn 1880 – 1980: Gnéithe den Stair Shóisialta*. Two short-story collections published, *Mac an tSagairt* and *An Fear a·Phléasc*, and first novel, *Sna Fir*, to be published shortly. Has won many national literary awards, particularly for his short stories, including the Butler Literary Award in 1997. He also won the Hennessy Award for Literature in 1997 and was nominated New Irish Writer of the Year.

DEATH AT A FUNERAL

It would have been ridiculous for Eamon Bartley to stay ensconced in his coffin any longer. He couldn't anyway. He was far too good to have died. Every one of the merry mourners at the funeral was praising him – praising him up and down and back to front and top to bottom and arse to elbow – even those who hated his guts once upon a time; those who had it in for him due to some old dispute; those who cursed him roundly and fucked him from a height; those who didn't talk to him for yonks; those who crossed the road to avoid him, or looked right when he was on the left, or who stared at the ground if he was all around them. Every man jack of them praising him with gusto now. They were mourning him and mourning him and mourning him, they sure were.

"Eamon was all right you know, the poor fucker."

"The whole town will miss him."

"You could depend on Eamon, a sound man."

"The poor soul, God love him."

"He was kind and helpful to everybody."

"He was all of that and more, even if he wasn't the full shilling."

"Too true."

"You never said a more honest word."

"Absolutely."

Eamon suddenly began to think that he'd be a proper fool to remain dead in his coffin any longer. Not one minute longer. Neither right nor proper nor appropriate. Besides it would be wrong to these good heart-broken people gathered around him. Maybe I'm confused, he thought to himself, or maybe I'm not the same person I was . . . in which case it wasn't me who knocked up Micil Bawn's young one at all; or broke into Mary Andy's shop and made off with two thousand pounds, or nicked the sugar lumps from the priest's tea the day he was around for the stations, or who crashed into Martin More's nice new car without tax or insurance, or who firebombed the co-op's offices when they sacked me, or who broke into the police station looking for my hooch which the bastards swiped . . .

With one vicious smash he crashed up through the brown coffin lid. Sat up. Straightened himself. As straight as a bamboo cane in a teacher's hand.

The mourners woke up in consternation from muttering their prayers. Some of them jumped out of their skins – and into others. A few of them gawped. Others seemed to run off in four directions at once as if they were doing a set dance mixed up with a waltz. The rest of them froze like icicles on a cold March day.

Eamon Bartley Coolan looked around him. And then looked slowly around him again in silence from person to person. His head and shoulders were barely up over the edge of the grave. He was grinning all over. A grin that grew until it went from ear to ear. A big, broad, stupid, crescent grin.

"Aren't you all happy that I'm alive and kicking again?" he said, buddy-like and upbeat. Then he stopped, expecting someone to say something, anything, even a stutter. But there was no answer, not a word. He broke the silence again. "Look, even though I liked the other life better than this miserable vale of tears, I just couldn't not come back, you missed me so much. You are all so nice, so straight. Too straight and honest really. I was really touched the way you guys all said nice things about me, praising me to the skies. Every single one of you. And I felt such pity for you. Your wailing and weeping would make the stones themselves burst into tears . . . and that's why I, that's why . . . hold on a minute . . . something wrong? . . . why are you all so quiet and gawking at me with your big wide eyes . . . do I detect some misgivings or what, now that I've thrown away the shroud . . . I mean, come on, it's a bit early for me to die again, isn't it . . . but on the other hand, of course, I wouldn't like to create difficulties for any of you lot. Begging your pardon then, my friends and companions and brothers in Christ, but am I allowed to stay just a little bit longer, to live just a little bit more? Am I?"

Nobody answered him at first. Nobody spoke. They stood around like statues, like telephone poles, like stiffened stalagmites. The priest. The undertaker. The doctor. The workers. His widow. The local petty politician who turned up at every funeral with his wet handshake.

Relations of all kinds. Some who had never been heard of, others who denied having anything to do with him. Toddlers and ragged urchins. Teenagers. Neighbours. People from the town. From the hills. The odd person that nobody knew . . .

– I drank fifteen pints at his wake. I'm tellin' ya. Fifteen bloody pints. I never sank my moustache into so many creamy pints, the very best of pints, for the sake of a scrounger who never spent one penny on a drink in his life, nor on anything else either until he died. Don't let him spoil our day's boozing now . . . Believe me, he doesn't deserve to live.

– I was certain he was dead. Absolutely sure. Didn't I feel his pulse? I put my hand on his pulse three or four times, and I felt his heart, his . . . No sign of life whatsoever. One hundred per cent sure. I'd be able to recognize a dead man rather than a live one any day before anyone else . . . I have years of practice . . . Think of my reputation, my good name, my professional record . . . I'm telling you, he doesn't deserve to live . . .

– The coffin is ruined anyway. Whoever heard of a second-hand coffin? And it smells. His name and date of death finely and clearly engraved on its brass plate, all arrangements on the news and in the papers. It's not as if it could be used again. You couldn't flog a pine overcoat that somebody had already worn. It would be unlucky, unhealthy. Think of the risk. Even a live person wouldn't be happy to sit into a second-hand coffin, never mind a second-corpse coffin, never mind a dead person . . . For God's sake, he doesn't deserve to live . . .

– He never voted for me. Never. Not once. The Bartleys always stuck with the other crowd, they didn't change over when some did the time of that bother about the pot-holes and the water. When I think of all the cars we sent to bring him to the polling booth on election day. Total waste of time. Election after election. And he never once voted for me after all I did for him. And I don't suppose he's going to change his mind now with another election coming . . . On mature reflection, he doesn't deserve to live . . .

– He was a nasty bastard anyway. Frightening the shite out of me on the road coming home from school. Trying to scare me. Acting the eejit. Talking about ghosts, and hobgoblins, and fairies, all those silly things that aren't there any more. Telling stupid stories. Acting the real prick. He bullied me often enough . . . I used to dirty the bed, not sleep at night, and have nightmares because of him . . . When you think about it he doesn't deserve to live . . .

– I put ten pounds offering on his altar. Ten pounds, boy. I did, I'm telling you. I sweated blood and tears for those ten pounds, and yet I gladly offered them up to the Divine Lord because he answered my prayers . . . that I wouldn't see him sneaking past my door again . . . he was a right one . . . and may God grant that he never comes snooping around again. If I had to offer another ten pounds on his altar I'd be completely bust. No way . . . If you ask me, he doesn't deserve to live.

– He was a liar. A consummate irredeemable liar. Pretending he had snuffed it. Making fools of people. Drawing attention to himself. Throwing shapes. Acting the big cheese. Trying to show the world that we in this town are only stupid pig-ignorant blubberbrains. Well, he has another think coming, he doesn't deserve to live . . .

– I came all of seventy miles to be here at his funeral. Seventy long Irish miles neither give nor take an inch or a half-inch. My health isn't good, you know. I'm ailing myself. I've put my life in danger by coming all the way here just to see him laid out. So I could see him stone-dead before my very own eyes. I just had to. OK, so I had a face on me and we weren't talking for a long time, but I wouldn't give the satisfaction of not coming to his funeral. Seventy miles, despite my bad health . . . my rheumatism, varicose veins, blood-pressure, weak heart . . . despite my . . . ah, what the hell, he doesn't deserve to live . . .

– I'd put a bet on with the bookie. Quite simple really. Five thousand pounds. Five thousand pounds that he wouldn't make it to the end of the week. Jaysus, I'd lose everything. My house, my car, my ex-wife, the whole bleedin lot . . . Keep the final curtain down until next week and I'll have claimed my money, and I'll have made it sing . . . No doubt about it, he doesn't deserve to live . . .

– It's not him at all. Some kind of evil spirit. Some kind of malevolent changeling that causes havoc if he doesn't get his own way. He's not of this world at all, I'm more than certain of that. How do we know that he's not the devil incarnate in some kind of disguise? The spawn of Satan. He was always an Antichrist. He hasn't come back for our good, I'll tell you that . . . he doesn't deserve to live.

– Pretending all the time that he was a bit simple. A bit gaga. Nobody at home, like. I suppose he thinks now that we believe that he was that simple that he couldn't tell he should stay pegged out the way he was like any decent corpse with a wisp of sense. Like any decent corpse with any respect for the unfortunate creatures he had left behind. Himself and his stupid, inane, asshole simplicity. A bad bastardy ball-brained bollux . . . Let's be fair, he doesn't deserve to live . . .

– I'll never get the widow's pension. Fat chance as long as that fat turd is around. I'll be disgraced and mortified again like the last time when he shagged off and they called me the "live man's widow". We can't let him get away with it again. It would be apalling, unjust. He's a cheating lying deceiver anyway – letting on he was dead, the little shite. That was below the belt. The lying scumbag. He got his just desserts. If he crapped out as cold meat, let him stay crapped out to push up daisies like any half-decent man. It's bad enough when someone is a sly chancer in this life, but when they come back from the dead to be a sly chancer again it's ten times worse. We've yapped on long enough about him . . . he doesn't deserve to live . . .

– I got to him just in time. Just in time to anoint him. I wouldn't have, of course, if I hadn't left my fine dinner to go cold on me. I certainly wouldn't. And he wouldn't have made his last sincere confession if it hadn't been for me. A true and genuine confession from the bottom of his heart . . . real soul-searching stuff. When he was fading away and his breath coming in short wheezy gasps, I said the Act of Contrition right into his ear. I did, I did that. And before my prayer could go through his thick head and out through the other ear – puff! – he popped off. Croaked. Out for the last count. But it didn't matter, I had forgiven him all his sins, even the very worst of them, every single one of them – and I can tell you they were many and varied . . . robbery, calumny, lies, cursing and swearing, blasphemy, lechery and whoring and whoring and lechering . . . Not to mention all the newfangled sins he had deliberately learned from the New Catechism. I'd be here until morning

. . . or beyond. By the time I was finished with him he was ready to go; as ready and as steady as a strong stone bridge, and maybe he was half-way across it on his journey to Paradise if the fool had only kept going . . . The next time, yes the next time, the unfortunate man may not be half as prepared. Maybe he'd be caught off guard, on the hop. And as regards the altar offerings, they were the biggest that I have ever seen for a deceased man in this diocese. He must have been held in the greatest respect, or the greatest disrespect as the case may be and people were relieved to see him gone. All those fivers, and tenners, and even a few twenties . . . and all the Mass cards . . . hundreds of them with a fiver stuck in them all. Enough money for half the devils in hell to buy their ticket to Heaven. I'd never be able to give them all back, never – I've already booked two fortnights in Bangkok, put a fat deposit on a new car . . . and why not? An extension wouldn't be good for him anyway. More time would be bad news. I'm only for his own good. His soul was as pure and as scrubbed-clean as the new marble on a memorial monument. He wouldn't be half as ready the next time – that is, if there is to be a next time. He couldn't possibly be as prepared as he was, or his soul as ready to meet his Maker. I mean, if I was to be called out again to anoint him, I couldn't really be expected to . . . I mean, how could I believe that kind of a call. Once bitten twice shy and all that. He'd be the worst for it, he'd be the one to suffer. Another sackload of sins accumulated, one blacker than the other. God's will be done. We're only for his own good. In the name of God and of His Blessed Mother, and for all our sakes and the sake of all the saints and the suffering holy souls in Purgatory who are in torment, but most of all for his own sake, I have to say to you . . . that . . . he doesn't deserve to live . . .

 – He doesn't deserve to live . . .

 – Do away with him . . .

 – Send him back to where he came from . . .

 – Finish the job . . .

 – Good riddance . . .

 – For once and for all . . .

 – For ever and ever . . .

 – Amen.

They beat his legs. Broke his bones. Twisted his arms. Tortured his limbs. Split his skull in two places. They smeared blood on his face, on every part of him. Tore out his hair. Ripped out one of his balls. Bruised him black and blue with their boots and kicking. Stabbed him with knives, stabbed him anywhere they could find unstabbed flesh. Children spat and snotted at him . . .

After that they blessed the body.

translated by Alan Titley

FATHER

How was I supposed to know what to do – once I'd told him? I'd never seen my da crying before. Even when mum died nine months ago in the accident, he never cried as far as I know. I'm sure of it because it was I brought him the bad news. And I was around the whole time, up to and after the funeral. It was my job to stay with him. His brothers and my mother's brothers – my uncles – made all the arrangements, shouldered the coffin. And it was the neighbours, instructed by my sisters, who kept the house in some order. There was a sort of an understanding – unspoken, mind you – that it was best I stay with dad since I was the youngest, the only one still at home all year round.

That's how I'm nearly sure he didn't shed a tear. Not in the daylight hours anyway. He didn't need his hanky even. Sure, he was all over the place, you could hardly get a word out of him. Long silences would go by and he just stared into the fire or out the kitchen window. But no tears. Maybe it was the shock. The terrible shock to his system. But then again, you wouldn't really associate tears or crying with my father.

That's why I was so taken aback. Mortified. Not just the crying. But the way he cried. In fact, you couldn't really call it crying – it was more like something between a groan and a sob stuck in his throat. Yes, a muffled, pained sigh of revulsion a few seconds long. You'd've thought he choked on it like one of those horrible pills the doctor gives you. And he didn't even look at me, except for a stray watery glance that skirred by when I told him; afterwards, it was like he was trying to hide his face from me, half of it anyway. It should've been easier for him in a way; but not for me, there was no way I could look him in the face, for all my curiosity. So, while he dithered about, I sat there like a statue – only for my body-heat. The breath was knocked out of him; and me. Then I realized that even his smothered cry – if it could be let out – was better than this silence. Maybe you could do something about the cry, if it happened. A deadly silence was unworkable, impossible, as long drawn-out and painful as a judgment. I felt all the time that he wasn't looking anywhere near me, even when he got his breath back and some speech.

"And you . . ." he said, as if the word stuck or swelled up in his throat until he didn't know if it was safe to release it or rather he hoped, perhaps, that I would say it – the word that had popped in his ears just now, a word he was never likely to form in his rural throat unless it was spat out in some smutty joke for the lads down the pub. A word there wasn't even a word for in Irish, not easy to find anyway . . . I forgot I hadn't answered him, carried away trying to read his mind when suddenly he repeated:

"Are you telling me you're . . ."

"Yes," I said, half-consciously interrupting him with the same reticence, unsure whether he was going to finish his sentence this time, or not.

"I am," I said again quickly, uncontrollably, trying for a moment to make up for the empty silence.

"God save us," he said. "God *save* us," he said again as if he had to drag the words individually all the way from Mexico. It seemed to me he wanted to say more, anything, an answer or just some ready-made platitude, a string of words to pluck from the silence.

"Do you see that now?" he complained, taking a deep sniff of the kitchen air and blowing it out again with force. "Do you see that now?"

He grabbed the coal-bucket and opened the range to top up the fire. Then he lifted a couple of bits of turf out of the 10-10-20 plastic bag beside the range and – breaking the last two bits in half over his knee to build up his corner of the crammed space of the open range – shoved it on top. The coal was too hot – and too dear, he'd say – plus it was hard to burn the turf sometimes, or get much heat out of it, especially if it was still a bit soggy after a bad summer . . . He took the handbrush off the hook and swept any powdery bits of turf on the range into the fire. He slid the curly iron frame back into place with a clatter and took another deep breath, focusing on the range.

"And have you told your sisters about this?"

"Yes. When they were home this summer; the night before they went back to England."

He stopped a moment, still half-stooped over the range. He opened his mouth, then closed it again, making no sound, like a goldfish in a bowl. He tried again and, still choked with emotion, managed a broken sentence:

"And your mother – did she know?"

"Dunno," I said. "Mothers know a lot more than they get told."

"They do, they do. God rest them." He blessed himself, awkwardly. "But fathers know nothing. Nothing until it's spelt out for them."

He was standing at the table filling an already full kettle with well-water from the bucket. He placed it on the range again as if he was making tea the way he did after milking-time. He always made tea with well-water, boiling it in the old kettle instead of using tap-water and the electric kettle unless it was early in the morning when he'd no time. It would save on the electric, he said. Even mum couldn't get him to change. She wanted rid of the range altogether since the electric cooker was more consistent, more dependable for everything – dinners, cooking, boiling, baking, heating milk for the calves . . . There's always the chance of a power-cut, he'd say whenever there was a storm or thunder. If the electric runs out, it'll come in handy. And any time it happened, he'd turn to us, delighted, and say: "Aren't you glad now of the old range?"

He lifted the poker. Opened the top door of the range. Plunged it in to stir up the fire, trying to draw some flames from the depths. When the embers didn't respond very well, he turned the knob at the top of the range somewhat clumsily, making the chimney suck up the flame. He poked the fire another couple of times, a bit deeper, trying to let the air through. Soon there were flames dancing, blue and red, licking the dark sods and fizzing and flitting over the hard coal, shyly at first but growing in courage and strength. He closed the door with a deep thud, turning the knob firmly with his left hand, and put the poker back in the corner.

"And what about Síle Jimí Beag?" he asked suddenly, as if surprised he hadn't asked about her earlier. "Weren't you going out with her a few years ago?" he said, a hint of hope rising in his voice.

"Yes . . . in a way," I stammered. I knew that was no answer but it was the best I could do just then.

"In a way," he repeated. "What do you mean? You were or you weren't. Wasn't she coming here for a year and God knows how long before that? Didn't she leave Tomáisín Tom Mhary for you?" He stared at the bars over the range.

"But I was only . . . only eighteen back then," I said, changing my mind. "Nobody knows what they want at that age, or where they're going," I added.

"But they do at twenty-two, it seems! They think they know it all at twenty-two."

"It's not that simple, really," I said, surprising myself at going so far.

"Oh, sure, it's not simple. It's anything but!"

He pushed the kettle aside and opened the top of the range again as if he was checking to see the fire was still lit. It was.

"I went out with her, because I didn't know – I didn't know what to do, because all the other lads had a girl . . ."

"Oh, you were . . ."

"I asked her in the first place because I had to take somebody to the school formal. Everyone was taking some girl or other. I couldn't go alone. And it would've been odd to take Máirín or Eilín. They wouldn't have gone anyway. I couldn't stay at home because I'd've been the only one in my class not there. What else could I do?" I said, amazed I'd managed to get that much out.

"How do I know what you should've done? Couldn't you just be like everyone else . . . that, that or stay home?" There was something about the way he said "home".

"I couldn't," I said, "not forever . . . It's not that I didn't try . . ." I thought it best to go no further, afraid he wouldn't understand.

"So that's what brings you up to Dublin so much," he said, glad to have worked that much out for himself.

"Yes. Yes, I suppose." What else could I say, I thought.

"And we were all convinced you had a woman up there. People asking me if we'd met her yet . . . or when we'd get to see her. Aunty Nóra asking just the other day when we'd have the next wedding . . . thinking a year after your mother's death would be OK."

"Aunty Nóra doesn't have to worry about me. It's as well she didn't get married herself anyway," I said, scunnered as soon as I'd said it at the suggestion I was making.

"Up to Dublin! Huh." He spoke to himself. "Dublin's quare and dangerous," he added, in a way that didn't require an answer.

He turned around, his back to the range. Clambered over to the kitchen table. Tilted the milk-cooler with his two hands to pour a drop of it into the jug till it was near overflowing. I was glad he never spilt any on the table, ready to clean it up if I had to. I felt awkward and ashamed sitting there watching him do this – my job usually. He poured the extra milk that wouldn't fit in the jug into the saucepan the calves used and set it on the side of the range to heat it up until the cows were milked; after that he'd see to the calves. He lifted the enamel milk-bucket that was always set on the table-rails once it was cleaned every morning after the milking. Then he gave it a good scalding with hot water from the kettle – water boiled stupid that had the kettle singing earlier. He set down the kettle, with its mouth turned in, back on the side of the range so that it wouldn't boil over with the heat. He swirled the scalding water around the bottom of the bucket and then emptied it in one go into the calves' saucepan. He stretched over a bit to grab the dishcloth off the rack above the range. Dried the bucket. Hung it up again rather carelessly, watching to see it didn't roll down on top of the range. It didn't.

All at once, he straightened up as if a thought had suddenly struck him. He turned round to me. Looked for a second as our eyes met and went over each other. The look he gave was different from the first – that soft sudden glance he gave me when I first told him. I noticed the wrinkles across his forehead, some curled, some squared off, the short grey hair pulled down in a fringe, the eyebrows: the eyes. What eyes! It was those eyes drove out of me whatever dream was going through my head just then. Those eyes caught me out all right. Those eyes that could say so much without him even having to open his mouth. I understood then that the only way to look at a man was right in the eyes, even if it was a casual side-glance, on the sly . . . I looked away, couldn't take any more, grateful that he took it upon himself to speak. He had the bucket tucked up under his armpit the way he did when he was going out milking.

"And what about your health?" he managed to say, nervously. "Is your health OK?"

"Oh, I'm fine, just fine," I replied quick as I could, more than glad to be able to give such a clear answer. I started tapping my fingers. Then it struck me just what he was asking.

"God preserve us from the like of that," he said over his shoulder to me, on his way to the door. You could tell he was relieved.

"You don't have to worry," I said, trying to build his trust, having got that far. "I'm careful. Very careful. Always."

"Can you be a hundred per cent careful?" he added curiously, his voice more normal. "I mean if half what's in the Sunday papers and the week's TV is true."

I let him talk away, realizing he probably knew much more than I thought. Wasn't the TV always turned towards him, with all sorts of talk going on in some of the programmes while he sat there in the big chair with his eyes closed, dozing by the fire it seemed but probably taking it all in.

He took his coat down off the back of the door, set it over the chair.

"And did you have to tell me all this at my age?"

"Yes and no." I'd said it before I realized, but I continued: "Well, I'm not saying I had to, but I was afraid you'd hear it from someone else, afraid someone'd say something about me with you there." I thought I was getting through. "I thought you should know anyway; I thought you were ready."

"Ready! I'm ready now all right . . . And are you telling me people round here know?" he said, disgusted.

"Yes, as it happens. You can't hide anything . . . especially in a remote place like this."

"And you think you can stay around here?" he exclaimed in what sounded to me like horror. His words hit home so quick I didn't know whether they were meant as a statement or a question. Did they require an answer: from me or himself, I wondered. Sure, I was intending to stay, or I should say, happy to stay. He was my father. I was the youngest, the only son. My two sisters had emigrated. It was down to me. Although my sisters had convinced me the night before they went away that there was always a place for me in London if I needed it.

Surely, he should've known I would want to stay. Who else would look out for him? Help with the few animals we had, look after the house, keep an eye on our wee bit of a farm, see he was all right, take him to Mass on Sunday, keep him company . . . "And you think you can stay around here," I wondered, none the wiser, still trying to work out whether I was to take it as a question or a statement; if he expected an answer or not.

He'd dragged his wellingtons over between the chair and the head of the table and was bent down struggling to undo the laces of his hobnailed boots. He looked different that way. If I had to go, I said to myself . . . If he threw me out and told me he didn't want to see me or have anything more to do with me . . .

Right away, I recalled some of my mates and acquaintances in Dublin. The ones that were kicked out by their families when they found out: Mark whose father called him a dirty bastard and told him not to come near the house again as long as he lived; Keith whose da gave him a bad beating when he discovered he'd a lover, and who kept him locked up at home for a month even though he was near twenty; Philip who was under so much stress he'd a nervous breakdown, who'd no option but to leave his teaching job after one of his worst pupils saw him leaving a particular Sunday-night venue and the news spread by lunch-time the following Monday. The boys called him disgusting names right to his face, never mind the unconcealed whispers behind his back. Who could blame him for leaving, even if it meant the dole and finding a new flat across town? The dole didn't even come into it for Robin . . . Twenty-four hours his parents gave him to clear out of the house and take all he had with him, telling him he wasn't their son, that he'd brought all this on himself, that they never wanted to see him again as long as he lived. Which they didn't. Coming home that night to find his body laid out on the bed in their room, empty pillboxes on his chest, half a glass of water under the mirror on the dressing-table, a short crumpled note telling them that his only wish was to die where he was born, that he loved them, and was sorry he hurt them but saw no other way.

The slow-rolling chimes of the clock interrupted my litany. He was still opposite me, working away trying to pull on his boots with great difficulty, his trousers tucked down his thick woollen socks. If I had to go, I thought, I'd never see my father like this again. Never. The next time I'd see him, he'd be stone-cold dead in his coffin, the three of us back together on the first plane from London after getting an urgent phone call from home telling us he was found slumped in the garden, or that they weren't sure if he fell in the fire or was dead before the fire burnt the house to the ground overnight, or maybe they'd find him half-dressed in the bedroom after some of the neighbours forced in the door, trying to work out when was the last time they saw him, no one able to work out exactly the time of death . . .

He'd got into his wellingtons and stood there wrapped up in his great coat, holding his cap, about to put it on, the enamel milk-bucket under his arm.

He moved slowly, tottered, almost, over to the front door. My eyes followed his face, his side, his back, his awkward steps away from me as his last words of a moment ago went round and round in my head like an eel scooped out of a well on a hot summer day and set on a warm stone.

He paused at the door the way he always did on his way out and dunked his finger in the holy-water font hung up on the door-jamb. It was an old wooden font with the Sacred Heart on it my mother brought back from a pilgrimage to Knock the time the Pope was over. I could see him trying to bless himself, not even sure if it was the finger or thumb he'd dipped in the holy water he was using.

He placed his hand on the latch. Opened it and pulled it towards him.

He turned round and looked at me, head first, his body following slowly. He was staring right at me which stopped my mind racing and swept my thoughts back to their dark corners.

"Will you stand by the braddy* cow for me?," he asked, "while I'm milking . . . she's always had a sore teat . . ."

---

* Irish bradach: thieving, trespassing

translated by Frank Sewell

SEVEN HUNDRED WATCHES

Somewhere in this city is a shop – if you could call it that – and it only opens one day in the year. Naturally enough this day never falls on the same date, since each year is a muddle of three hundred and sixty five days. Of course as to this particular shop, very few are in the know and the cognoscenti keep it to themselves. They really don't give a hoot about it and care little who does as long as they are not reminded of it. They steer clear of it.

They know what they are about, or like to believe so. They are indifferent. Maybe you are too, if you're anything like them. I am far from indifferent. I went in there once, on an impulse, propelled by my own two feet, on a chance visit to the city. That's why I'm no longer indifferent and if, perchance, you find yourself there some day, you too will be indifferrent no longer. I'm still there you see – I'm here: I'm waiting for you . . .

I was on a visit to the city, a walkabout. One of those mindless days with nothing grabbing my attention, not a living thing. You know the way it is. Loafing about, unsure about the universe, down one street, up another and sometimes half-way down a street that I had walked five minutes previously before the onset of vague *déjà vu*. You could say I was in a trance-like state with a hint of ennui. You can be certain sure that it's easier to find yourself in the metropolitan maze than to get out of it, as a rustic philosopher remarked in days gone by. And I continued my saunterings. Now and again I would stop and stare at a window, checking a price before deciding it was beyond my reach, examine an item of furniture that I did not require, give ear to distant Muzak pouring from a premises. Such were my vacant ways on that shambolic day. My mind was free or perhaps astray, half-dreaming, half-conjuring things up and, fleetingly, in a state of no-mind.

And yet I was happy for reasons unknown to me. The world was my oyster – ay, ay, sir – until I wended my way down a cul-de-sac, at the end of which stood a shop with its small yellow door. At first I failed to distinguish its name and, pressing closely, discovered it had none, something that excited my curiosity. Nothing at all in that murky window but an old-fashioned clock that had stopped long ago, a clock you'd never find today except in a disused convent or an antique store. Yes, I said to myself, there might be something here and as I had a few hours of the afternoon to idle away, in I went. The door creaked as I entered. I've never liked proclaiming my entrance or attracting the attention of shopkeeper or assistant – especially if I had no intention of buying anything.

Snakes alive! Not a sinner in sight. The hovel contained hundreds of watches, crouched on shelves and counters and, when space had run out, dangling from the ceiling . . . hundreds, maybe thousands of watches . . . They were a mystery to behold and those that still functioned played their part as though in an orchestra of crickets – little twelve-eyed insects in most unnerving harmony. Each had its own dignity and I noticed how jealously they preserved their own space, their luminous integrity. I was *watching* each and every one, from row to row, from shelf to shelf, up down, down up. I was in a state of total non-communication with myself for a considerable period, absorbing all within the range of my vision.

The world was a pulsing watch. The previous world had stopped. I took courage, grabbed a watch and examined it.

"It's yourself!" I startled. I turned around to see whose voice it was . . .

He was leaning over the counter, hands propping his face. From my vantage point he appeared to be a hunchback, but he might have been different had he stood erect. He was a wizened, triangular-skulled creation, a blue-rinsed mop that was in need of a hayfork, protruding black eyebrows like some remote bramble-bush and the wrinkled face on him could only be likened to the skin of an anorexic elephant's ears. My immediate impulse was to laugh and to ask him did his hair know what a comb was. I didn't, of course. He was not a pleasing sight – but I didn't inform him of this. Would you?

"Just browsing," I said, picking up another watch with feigned interest. His face was a thousand times more interesting than that of the watch. When next I raised my head he had his back turned to me – rather rudely I thought – and appeared to be winding a watch. I picked up another watch, and yet another. I noted their shape, colour, make, weight and sound. I was amazed at how little interest he had in me, fumbling and toying with his watches, behind the counter. I spied him out of the corner of my eye. When he had wound one of them he would lay it aside, look around, pause and pick up another, and yet another and another again. He continued thuswise for quite some time. I was sure he would call me and persuade me to buy one as is the wont with his type, but strange as it may seem, I might not have been there at all as far as he was concerned as he pottered around picking watches that needed winding. This pleased me no end as I have a distaste for those callous salesmen who would persuade a corpse to buy life insurance. He might have been a grotesque figure but at least he let me alone to browse among the watches . . .

Time flew as I watched them, admiring their variety. Something, I felt, was needling me – do you know not one of them had a price-tag and, more remarkable still, no pair told the same time. This only fuelled my curiosity. I looked again, here and there, but sure enough not one synchronized with the other. I wonder, I reflected, are they all in competition, in a race, or jealously guarding their own time and space – independent of each other? Or are they all part of a team that ensures that every living second is covered? If that be the case they're having me on and everybody else to boot – except that it appears that anyone with a grain of sense steers clear of this place. But why, I asked myself, if they are able to keep time, as dutiful watches, why have they all gone wonky, if wonky they be? Or is it me? It's often difficult to distinguish between the normal person and one with a question mark over him. Practically the same . . .

But speaking of time, what hour of the day is it, I asked myself and looked at my watch. Quarter to two. Quarter to shit! It must have stopped. I put my wrist to my ear. Dead as a dodo. I shook my hand. Again. The bastard had stopped, to be sure. Now what would I do, not being able to tell the time, surrounded by a flock of watches and not one of them you could trust, going by their antics. If I approached Quasimodo he'd try to sell me a watch for sure, and who could blame him? Already he was squinting at me as though he sensed I had a dilemma.

"You are bereft of time," he muttered, putting a watch aside and taking up another. I agreed. What else could I do?

"Had you looked after it well," said he, "it wouldn't have let you down."

"What looking after? All a watch needs is winding. It's not an infant that needs its botty oiled twice a day!"

"Ah, were it as simple as that," he sighed, shaking his head heavily and looking at another watch. "I speak you see, not of the watch, but of time."

No, I'm not going to argue with him, I told myself. He seemed the debating type and that was the last thing on my mind. I'd think of an excuse to be off.

"What time is it anyway?" I asked politely.

"What time do you require?"

"What do you mean what – " and my hackles were beginning to rise, "what, pray is the hour?"

"Right now?"

"Yes, yes, this instant!" There was tension in my voice.

"But that depends on the time you require."

"I do not require – "

"But didn't you ask – ?"

"I merely asked you for the time because I need to know."

"And what need have you any more of time?"

"Is that any concern of yours?"

"Whether it is or no, I do not give of my time, gratis, to all and sundry not knowing beforehand what need they have of it."

"Your time?"

"My time, yes. Isn't that what you want?"

"The time is yours, I suppose."

"If it's not, why are you asking me?"

"Now look here, sir!" I was agitated by now and I'm sure it was clear from my voice. "I simply require the time. If you are not prepared to give it, fine – but say so. If you are prepared, give it to me now and no more shite and onions, OK?"

"But how can I give you something which you already have . . .?"

"I don't have the fuckin' time and – "

"Not knowing the reason you require it, since you refuse to tell me."

"OK, why do I require it, why do I require the time . . . because my wife has an appointment with the dentist at three o'clock."

"Your poor wife has an appointment with the dentist at three o'clock?"

"Yes, to extract a rotten tooth, if you most know and I must get home and drive her to the dentist."

"And are you certain sure . . . that the rotten tooth is not yours?"

I grabbed an old clock from the table beside me and decided if I got hold of him I wouldn't leave a tooth, rotten or sound, in his head.

"Waste of time trying to knock a tooth out of me with that clock," he remarked, "since all I've got is plastic false teeth and not one of them rotten, as false teeth do not decay. Anyway I keep them clean, but I'll tell you the time if you have an appointment . . . "

"My wife I told you, at three o'clock." I put the clock aside and retreated a step or two.

He looked around, paused, and looked around again. Then he stretched out his hand and picked up a watch in front of him.

"Well then, it's three o'clock," he said, nonchalantly, peeking over his spectacle frames.

"What's this *well then*? That watch isn't right."

"Every single watch here is in order," he stated, somewhat sternly. "It's you that's out of order. Every watch here has the right time. Don't insult my watches!"

"The right time, eh?"

"Be sure of it, with the exception of that nonsensical trinket on your wrist which has no time at all – except time that has ceased – and that isn't time at all."

I was becoming stressed out again. No, not stress; frenzy, feverish frenzy. And yet, somehow, I managed to restrain myself.

"And let us say," said I, attempting to put this ridiculous ball into his own court, "let us say my wife's appointment was for four."

"With the dentist . . . the rotten tooth."

"Never mind the tooth . . . if the appointment was for four, it would be four o'clock now according to your way of looking at things."

"The way the world looks at things, not me. But you're perfectly correct," he said. "I'm glad you're getting a glimmer of things at last."

I didn't answer him. What was the point? No sense arguing with this fellow at all. For the sake of peace I'd buy a watch – that might shut him up – and hightail it out of this joint.

He had gone back to his watches. In a fit I took off my own watch. I gave it a good rattle but if a million earthquakes erupted under its navel it wouldn't come to life. I looked around once more at the watches until I picked one that looked user-friendly enough. I'd buy it if it were at all reasonable. He would put the right time on it, hopefully, and I would make my escape.

"Excuse me," I said, to attract his attention.

"Oh, you're still there," he said, feigning surprise. "Thought I heard you slipping out a while ago."

"I'll buy a watch," I said, handing it to him, "if the price is right."

"No can do," he said with a churlish shake of the head. "None of the watches here is priced."

"What?"

"Not one; do you not get it yet? Time isn't for sale. When are people going to stop buying and selling? They'll never learn." He shook his head gravely. Sorrow had invaded his face.

"You're saying that the watches here are not for sale?"

"Oh, none of these watches will ever be sold. You don't think you're in some terrestrial shop, do you?"

I didn't know what to do. I looked into his two eyes, trying to figure out what kind of a son of a gun he might be. If I'd taken a few pints I'd have smashed his face in before he knew what time it was. It was difficult to know whether to sympathize or to be angry with him but it was becoming plain that there was little point in locking swords with him.

"If it's not a shop what is it?" I asked with as much civility as I could muster.

"Don't you realize," says he pretending to be astonished, "that it's merely a waiting-room for watches, watches like you and the world."

"Like me? Waiting for what?" I asked, while telling myself I might as well humour him if we were going to get to the bottom of this.

"Oh, that I can't say," he retorted; "such a ponderous question you should ask yourself, or the watches, but it's unlikely that they would satisfy you with an answer. The whole world's waiting and we haven't a clue what we're all waiting for . . . "

"I see," I said. It was balderdash, of course. "And you can't sell me any of these watches?"

"It's not right to sell," he said sombrely and sorrow had once more invaded his being. "Selling is not right and people are breaking the law ten days a week. I'm sure you've seen them. Advertisements everywhere. Selling, selling, selling and earmarking everyone! Some of them sell the same things twice and even three times. Others sell stolen property, or stuff that isn't theirs to sell, and more of them sell themselves – soul and body." He drew a breath. "Nothing to do with me," says he, "as long as you're not one of them . . . But there's one good thing you can sell," says he, and I could see he was chuffed by the attention I was paying to his rant; "your watch is kaput but you can sell it to me and I'll only ask you for twenty pounds."

I was nonplussed. I drew a breath. It took me a while to figure out his offer. I felt like the bird in the cuckoo-clock with a dose of laryngitis:

"I can . . . I can sell my own watch . . . to – to you," I stammered, "and throw in twenty quid while I'm at it? That would leave me minus my banjaxed watch and minus twenty pounds. What sort of a deal is that? That's robbery, mate – daylight robbery!"

"It mightn't sound like a good deal to someone who's a bit astray but it's the right deal for you at this point in your life. Right now, this minute! And I'll set your watch going again. Isn't that what you want?"

Like a big eejit – and to this hour I don't know what prompted me – I took out my last twenty-pound note and handed it to him, with the watch. And do you know what? I was rather pleased with the transaction.

He took the watch, without looking at it. Instead he looked at all the other watches in his den – those on shelves and tables, those dangling from the ceiling and his beady eye roamed from one to the other.

"Got it," he said finally with a wink, his mouth breaking into a smile, a twinkle forming in his eye. "I've discovered a time previously unknown, a time that no other watch has. How fortunate you are!" The smile had crept fully across his mouth. He fixed the time on the watch-face and opened up the back. Taking a little plastic bag from his jacket pocket he picked out what appeared to be a tiny white tablet. This 'he crushed into powder between his thumb-nails and deposited the dust into the watch's womb.

"Now," says he, "that'll keep you going for a good while – maybe forever. " He closed the back of the watch and shook it close to his ear, as though concocting a cocktail.

A fog descended on my brain. The two of us looked at the watch. The hands were at it like blazes, scything away for all their worth. My heart rose.

"Now," says he, "do you see that! Do you hear it? The purring of a kitten that's got the cream."

"What was that white stuff you put into it?"

"Do you not know? What galaxy are you from at all? That's crack lad, the hottest dope around. Mighty big in America, as they say, and it's cheap too."

"And you're peddlin' dope to these wretched watches?" I said, looking all around me and my eyes beginning to water almost.

"That's all they want, lad. It's the dope that keeps them ticking over – sure isn't it keeping the whole world going? Sure yeah, all these watches are doped to the gills, high as kites . . . some are stoned on cannabis, others on coke, more on grass, a lot on E, LSD, speed, ice – the lot. Crack's the latest."

"They like the crack?"

"Mad for it. Wired to the moon half of the time, hyperactive, schizophrenic, zonked, but full of devilry and the joys of life – can't you see yourself all twelve eyes of them popping out of their heads – and the way their hands are going, the fast lane, eh? None of them at the same speed, none having the same time and that's the way they like it and that's the way the world should be. Boring old farts they are not, or feckless fools going around imitating each other – but they have a certain rustic pigheadedness and humanity about them and if they're not having a good time I don't know who is."

"And you're the one who keeps them going?"

"Myself and God's spirit. Oh, it's hard work I'm telling you. My perspiration alone would fill buckets." He picked up another watch. "Winding and winding. We do our best. What else can anyone do? A lot depends on us. Trying to get the time, keeping the time going, putting in time, stopping time, seizing the hour from time to time whenever possible. Time and tide wait for no man, time belongs to no one and we only have it on loan, to keep going as long as we can, as long as we can . . . "

"And it's here that time and all the time in the world is kept going?"

"It's all here. All time resides here – and simple folk think there's nothing going on here. They haven't the time to come in even. They haven't time to do this or time to do that. Nobody has time any more for God or man or beast, not to mention time for time. The poor ignorant savages. They avoid this place, poor things. If they only knew that all time is encapsulated here. Anyone who finds himself here hasn't the time or the inclination to leave. And there's loads of time here for anyone who wants to come looking for it – if they only knew. They wouldn't have to do anything else again for the rest of their lives – simply pause for a second outside the door and slink in – as you did."

"As I did?"

"Oh, yes, lad, as you did."

translated by Gabriel Rosenstock

THE MAN WHO EXPLODED

Where exactly did it happen, is that what you're asking, is it? Right smack bang in the middle of the street, Joe, that was it, smack bang in the middle of the street. The upper main street that juts out from the square in the guts of the city. Where else did you think? Are you right or are you right? All the action happens all the time in the guts of the city. He wouldn't have bothered his arse exploding way out in the suburbs, and why would he? That would have been the end of it. No more said. Waste of time.

Saturday afternoon? That's what I said, Saturday afternoon when the place is busy as hell. Shagging shoppers! Shagging shoppers, Joe, with things to do and their shagging kids off school. And half of the hill-billies in from the mountains with shag-all left to do except make some use of their free travel. Finding out who else was in and about. Bad news, Joe, bad news. He picked a lousy time to explode, I'll say that much. He could have really fucked things up, he could've. Standing out there in the middle of the road like a statue. And then, boom! Traffic screwed up for the rest of the day. Traffic jams everywhere. Time to duck, I'd say. It wouldn't have been so bad early in the morning, or late at night, or even on Sunday apart from Mass-time . . .

A warning? What do you mean "a warning"? Warning my arse, Joe, cop yourself on. People who are going to blow the shite out of themselves hardly give a warning. Why should they? It's part of the game, man, part of the show, part of the miraculous mystery of the big bang. Anyway, if he gave a warning nobody would have seen him, would they? Nobody there to tell the tale. Everyone fucked off like snots off a shovel. Fucked off like hares with gas up their arse. Not a twit nor a twat left on the street. What you say? Winos? OK winos if you like. Winos or quarehawks trying to take the balls out of his eyes or the change from his pockets if he had any . . . or the police, or the army if they bothered to come out to defuse him . . . and I don't suppose they'd bother. What the hell could they do anyway? What could they do to stop some guy determined to blow himself to kingdom-come? Who ever trained them for chrissake? How can you have an expert who knows how to decommission some knob for blowing yourself up? And then if he went wham bang just when they were fiddling with him, if he got them right between the eyes and under the oxter. The army experts were clueless, also. I suppose they had a lot more important work to do. Anyway, a man isn't the same as a bomb. You're right there Joe, you could take the harm out of a bomb easily enough, but a man, a person . . . even the American Army itself couldn't take the harm out of a person, never mind defuse them . . . Isn't that why he exploded without warning . . . Oh, he was a tricky Dicky all right, slick enough to make no excuses to nobody.

Stuck a pin up his arse, is that what you're saying? I don't believe that. Hate that. They made a hole in his arse with the jab of a pin and he went up in splinters? Ah come off it, cop yourself on Joe. That's all balls. Bollix. Pig's bollix hanging down. Don't believe those crap artists, Joe, I'm telling you. That's all me eye and Betty Martin. Some chancer made that one up. It's only pub-talk. Bar-blather, pub piss-take. What do you mean, everyone says so? Doesn't one thing lead to another, a lie for a lie and a truth for a truth. For chrissake he wouldn't blow up like that if they made a hole in his arse. Come off it, cop yourself on. Wasn't there a hole there already, there had to be. A hole so big that the sun shone out of it, some people said. But, hang on, that's not a nice story. Forget I ever said it. But one way or the other, Joe, he was a man and not a baloon before he exploded. A man like any other man. A man first and foremost. Even if he exploded because he swelled up like a balloon, he was still a man for all that . . .

Internal pressure? Maybe so, Joe, maybe so. Could have been too much pressure. You know what I mean, him swelling up . . . expanding, getting bigger, like something boiling, bubbling over and not being able to hold himself. Oh, I suppose you're right Joe. Had to happen sooner or later. Gave way at the sides and was ripped apart. Of course he couldn't have stood that god-damn pressure another second. Even a solid stone statue would have gone up under that strain. And booze? Go on, say it straight out, Joe. There's no doubt that the booze had something to do with it also. Doesn't it always. Drink is always involved in cases like this, wherever there's trouble and aggro you'll find the drink. But I suppose he did have some kind of excuse, however small. I suppose he did, Joe. Wouldn't things be properly fucked up if he exploded for no reason whatsoever . . . ?

Did he have a job? Is that what you're asking, Joe? I didn't hear that he had. Is a man a real man if he has no job? They say he had none anyway, that he didn't want one, but that doesn't mean he was idle . . . Some arty-farty thing they say. Messing around with art? OK working with art, Joe. An artist if you like, in fact, he was quite an important artist if some of the reports are to be believed. Others denied that, of course. Don't they always. There you have it again. As many begrudgers as you have arse-lickers. Now don't ask me why. I don't understand this caper any more than anyone else. I'm as ignorant as the rest in these matters. But whatever kind of art he was up to he was always doing . . . doing queer things. I'm telling ya, really weird things . . . things that made no sense . . . things that were useless, some people said. One way or the other anyway, Joe, listen I'll tell ya . . . this Yank bloke comes to him one day and buys a tree . . . a feckin' Papal cross. Ah no, Joe, forget that Papal cross, that's all shite . . . look you eejit, this one was made out of wire, one he made himself. So this American Yankee bloke buys this tree made of wire, not just any old kind of wire, but shaggin' barbed wire, imagine that. Barbed wire just like that spiky stuff around a prison wall. Pots of money! O you're right there, Joe. What else. They say he got dollops of dollars for his tree of wire . . . something you wouldn't get for a shaggin' Papal cross even if it grew. No way José. Now what do you make of that?

Jaysus, imagine having a forest of wire . . . you'd be a millionaire in a year, a bloody millionaire, man. Somebody said that a wire tree grew in America, that there are wire trees growing all over the place there. Could be too. Now what do you say, Joe? Leave it to the Yanks, boy. They'd grow anything, even a bloody strand of seaweed out in space . . . Now isn't that weird, the great artist's tree of wire. But that's what done for him too. Went to his head in the end. If it wasn't for his art and his wire tree he'd never have exploded. Many trees have fallen . . . but how many people have exploded?

Too true, Joe, too true. Could be that his head got too big for him. It happens . . . happens when people become famous. That's what happened, maybe. The pressure. That's it, the pressure and the fame and all that goes with it. Looking over his shoulder all the time at the other artists nibbling at his arse. It wasn't enough for him to be famous. He wanted to be bigger than the whole shebang of them put together. There they were always before him, haunting him. On the streets. Every corner of the town where you could stand or sit making way for themselves to lie down . . . thrown down in a dirty heap . . . as if they owned the place . . . giving each other airs and graces and rewards . . . selling themselves and their art before anyone else. All eyes on them, Joe. Huge crowds milling about them from the bank manager to the yobbo – examining their art, praising it as if they knew something about it, saying it was great for them to be there, that they added life to the city . . . and you wouldn't mind only most of them are only . . . only . . . piss artists. That's it Joe, you took the words clean out of my mouth. Piss artists. Don't dirty your mouth again with the word, that's it. Didn't one of them even claim that the stream of piss on the side of the road that his mangy shitty dog did – the one who was always crawling after him – was modern art. He stuffed it down his throat. That's what put so much air in him. No wonder he exploded with spite to get out of the way of that lump of street garbage, that lot who were robbing him of his reputation for their own glory. Maybe he just had to explode . . . just to start again, to get back his own sense of self-worth, to know who the fuck he really was. To make art of himself, every friggin' bit of him, that's what they said, to make himself into art . . . and then to explode. Without warning, without sweet whack all smack bang in the middle of the city streets . . . it was then they called what he had done modern art. I'm telling you they did. They accepted him then when they got it straight up the arse, or in the face, whichever you prefer. They had no other choice anyway when he was fucked up in a billion pieces. By Jaysus they didn't, Joe. Now they have him all lock, stock and barrel. They can keep him, they can fuckin' keep him.

And they did. Maybe if they didn't want him when he was alive they had no choice but to take him when he was plastered all over the place in bits and pieces. Every bit of the city got their own bit up their arse and in the nose and down their throat when chunks of his fat slob body were fucked around every building site and every arse-hole street in the arse-hole of the arse-hole city. By Jaysus, they had to put up with him then, Joe, I'm telling you that – a blob of guts here, a chunk of gob there, a toe or a finger or whatever, a bit of liver splattered on a lamp-post, a bit of an ear stuck on to the graveyard gate, a few fingernails half-stuck in the door of the National Theatre, a smidgen of lung smarmed on the goal-posts of the football field ... perched on the peak of the top of the cathedral one of his balls – that's a good one for you, they hadn't found the second one yet, crowds messing around as if they were on a treasure hunt . . . somebody said there was somebody from some American sperm bank sniffing around . . . that the blue-rinse crowd of frustrated American women were looking for a good deal. I mean, Jaysus, the great artist's sperm! . . . Probably too late, Joe, probably too late . . . Half his prick shot off on the top of the convent wall . . . the only two young nuns in the place pissing themselves laughing, the old nuns shrivelled up in their surprise and good fortune . . . asking the Archbishop to bless the place again from top to bottom and to keep two holy vigils one after the other . . . a sliver of his heart landed on some bank sub-office, one of his eyes came down smack plop on the Mansion House, just as you'd expect, a gobbet of his arse thrown up on the dole office where he collected his money every Tuesday, a shred of his foreskin stuck to the Garda barracks – they were looking for fingerprints in case of foul play . . . a wedge of his skull on the roof of the lab of the university . . . they were drawing up charts already hoping to make some use of them. Bad story, Joe, sad story. Anyway, as for the rest of him, I don't suppose anyone would know the difference, mounds of muscle, bits of bone, blobs of blood, whorls of water, brickbats of bone, strips of skin . . . gobbets of gollops of dollops plastering whole segments of the city – street and lamp-posts, and telephone boxes, and bus stops, and zebra crossings, and advertising hoardings, and shop-fronts, and schools, and statues of martyrs . . . you'd hardly say that any shaggin' bit escaped Joe, nothing at all, only maybe a bit of a backstreet or a hole of a public toilet . . . certainly some of the women's toilets escaped they said . . . maybe he was a ladies' man after all . . .

Some queer sight. The way they left him there. Even the dogs of the city weren't willing to go near him. They weren't willing to go near him even though their guts were hanging through their balls with hunger. I suppose an artist's cantankerous flesh, especially one who exploded, isn't the same as everybody else's mortal flesh. Dogs didn't eat nothin' after that, no other meat. Some wag said they were becoming veggies . . . going around with their noses in the air like snobby shites.

It was said, of course, that he should be put back together again . . . They could stitch him up, they said, if they got all the pieces in one place. Maybe the government could squeeze some slush-fund European grant and get some unemployed FÁS people . . . to like, stitch him so he'd grow together again . . . It was said, Joe, it was, but what else hasn't been said . . . A small oriental little fart of a doctor up in the hospital who might be able to blow some life back into him. He's miraculous. Maybe yes and maybe no . . . Sure thing, Joe, but I'd put my money on the second maybe. Maybe they should have tried it anyway. You never know. But they didn't. No more than Humpty-Dumpty in his day . . . The bigwigs of the Corporation voted unanimously against it. It was said that they did it out of fear . . . they were scared shitless that he'd wreck the joint if he was alive again . . . And anyway he was worth three times more scattered around the place dead. But between the two of us there was even another reason, Joe. Insurance! Millions of pounds in insurance that could never be claimed if he was alive again. That's one for ya! But that wasn't the official version, of course. The Corporation scumbags said that it would have been unfair to the artist. It was his own decision to blow up at that particular time and place – that he was opening a new chapter in the story of art in the city, and of course, in his own inimitable personal style. A conscious pre-planned decision, they said. A climax all of his own choosing. Some people would do anything, Joe . . . Sometimes they would . . . looking for recognition and publicity. His name in the next edition of the *Guinness Book of Records*. And wasn't he finally recognized in his own native city as a result. Isn't that something in itself? Twice refused the Freedom of the City during his life, and now he gets it despite the lot of them with a bit of violence. That was it, boy, that was it. All he ever wanted from the beginning, if they'd only have given it to him . . . Recognition . . . Exhibition . . . A Grand Exhibition . . .

A live grand exhibition of himself – and he dead! Hundreds of pieces of art that couldn't be valued, nor bought nor sold because they were priceless. There they were presented to the city. Real modern art, Joe, the genuine article, made from his own natural resources. The Junior Minister for Arts, Culture and the Breac-Ghaeltacht was summoned home from his sunny holidays to officially open the exhibition – while the stuff was still fresh, they said. Ordered home, I'm telling you he was. Accompanied by government officials just in case. The Minister said that the entire city outdoors was now one gigantic and ornamental gallery. That no developer or demolisher could touch a brick of a building from now on. Now, wasn't that worth it! His fame spread far and wide beyond these shores . . . great tourist potential and money-spinner for the entire region. Would bring thousands of interested visitors . . . he said it, Joe, he did . . . Double-deck buses full of tourists disgorging themselves into the shops . . . Small Japanese with their hand videos. Fat-arsed middle-aged American women with their spyglasses. Tall blonde German beasts with their cameras clicking . . . Trained guides showing them the city from open-topped buses. It's true, Joe, leave it to the tourists. Would be easy to satisfy them. Or to fool them. But the experts, Joe, the experts! They're the crowd to watch. Standing on one another's toes trying to make sense of it all . . . Every specialist and expert in the country – in the world, if it comes to that, pathologists, psychologists, pseudologists, sociologists, anthropologists, geologists, gayologists, arseologists, pissologists . . . After all, it isn't everyday that someone just blows up. Wasn't that what they said. Everyone for himself making sense of it in his own way . . . research for some of them, lectures around the world for others, money-spinning books, television appearances . . . More guards needed twenty-four hours a day or they'd cream off whole blobs of him in little plastic bags as samples . . .

Is that true, Joe? They're going to build a monument to him? Jaysus, that's a new one. Nothing to stop them of course. And why wouldn't they? Just across from where he blew up on the edge of the square? The Minister allowing twenty thousand pounds already from some special fund nobody knew nothing about until now? And the church matching them pound for pound? Two church collections and a special big collection at the church gates every Sunday? How's that for ya? How's that for ya when you think how short we all are of money. Maybe the Pope himself will come to Ireland again to unveil it? The holy Joes trying to claim him as one of their own now, are they? A martyr to the cause. They'll make a shrine to him underneath the monument thanks to the Corporation. They'll canonize him yet, will they? A cardinal or an archbishop on his way from Rome researching the case already. Then we'd have our own saint. We would, Joe, if you like that kind of thing. People being cured . . . Rumours going around that miracles were about to happen, just to be patient . . . any day now. Keeping an eye on people in wheelchairs and other invalids sentenced to death by disease. The clergy claiming that all the bits were holy relics. The nuns would have to stop their perennial prayers and come out of their convents to feed the hungry hordes coming on pilgrimage to the shrine – their backs broken stuffing them with chips and hot dogs. A string of rent-a-loo cabins like a rosary around the square to be kept sanctifyingly white for health reasons. Overflowing despite the charge for their use. Nice fat profits accumulating for the nuns to be spent on the black babies.

What's that, Joe? You didn't see the guy who exploded? That's bloody odd in itself. Everybody else saw him, even people who weren't there, people who weren't even in the city that very day. They saw him, I'm telling ya – or at least they said they did. Unless of course they saw him on TV that night, it was on all the news bulletins – and then they thought they were there, that they actually saw him go up in bits – you know the way it is, Joe, memory playing tricks with people, especially nowadays, virtual reality and all that. Too true, Joe, too true. So it goes. There are people and they'd see anything at all. They're there though. Drug addicts and junkies. People shooting themselves up day and night. They'd easily see someone who exploded even if they were never there themselves. Now you're talking. Druggies would see anything – Puff the magic dragon living by the sea and floating off somewhere over the rainbow . . . They'd swear black and blue that they did. And they'd be worse fools who swallowed their story. Who'd be first to believe it, Joe . . .

But I'm horrified to think that you of all people didn't see him . . . a sensible guy like you who sees everything and wouldn't let the grass grow under his feet. I have to say I thought you saw him, that everyone saw him . . .

Just so. Isn't that what I say all the time, Joe. Don't see anything you don't want to see and is none of your business. Keep your nose clean. It'll be seen anyway, despite yourself.

But you'd recognize him anyway if you spotted him, wouldn't you? You mean you're not sure? What do you mean you're not fuckin' sure? I'd be amazed if you didn't recognize a guy who exploded – much the same as any of us really, except he's blasted into tiny little bits . . . I find it really strange to think that you didn't see him Joe . . . really and truly . . . I was sure that every Tom, Dick and Harry in this city saw him. Everyone except myself.

translated by Alan Titley

PÁDRAIC BREATHNACH

Born in Moycullen, Co. Galway, he is now a lecturer in Irish in Mary Immaculate College at the University of Limerick. He is a novelist, essayist and short-story writer. Probably the most prolific short-story writer in Irish, having published over 150 such compositions to date. Renowned as a stylist, nature lover and for his depiction of youth.

His published works include *Bean Aonair* (1974), *Na Déithe Luachmhara Deiridh* (1980), *Gróga Cloch* (1990), *Taomanna* (booklet & cassette), *Íosla agus Scéalta Eile* (1992), *The March Hare* (1994) and *An Pincín agus Scéalta Eile* (1996) and *As na Cúlacha* (1998).

A BUCKET OF POTEEN

Were it not that Uncle Eoin, my father's brother, had come home and were it not that my family were all away in my Aunt Sorcha's house, she being ill, it's certain I wouldn't be in Danann Mharcais's house, the distiller, up in the grasslands of Tamhnachaí Arda. Not that night anyway. Or any other night. My family were rarely away.

They were trying to persuade me to go to my aunt's as well. I was told it was my duty to go there after how kind and generous she had been to us all. But what attraction had my aunt or her house for me, particularly at this time of the year? Now if it were summertime I could go hunting or fishing; I could go filching flowers and saplings for my own garden, but there was nothing doing this time of the year. There wouldn't even be sweet cake – Aunt Sorcha confined to bed, most likely, and my mother in charge of the meals. I was sure it would be the same awful fare as always: wholemeal bread and country butter. "Roma will be there!" said my mother, hoping that might entice me. Roma! God save us, who would want to play with the likes of her – that foolish, senseless girl! Let Peigí and Treasa play with her, and Andrew as well – but I was grown up! Anyway, I couldn't stand Roma and all her fancy notions: the hoity-toity voice, always neat as a pin, and her "Ladybird" books.

"Do you know what a stork is?"

She spoke authoritatively, like a schoolmistress, turning her head in a sophisticated manner, like a plover. She looked me straight in the eye and you'd swear that the insults were building up in her. She wouldn't wait long for an answer. "I know!" she said, proudly. "The stork is a member of the heron family . . ."

What was she on about, the little wretch. So cocksure of herself! I knew more about birds than she'd learn in a lifetime and let her not think differently. I knew more about animals, insects and whatever than she'd ever know. Did she know about the crane-fly? What did she know about the devil's coach-horse? Did she know anything outside of those "Ladybird" books of hers? Wouldn't any *amadán* know that the stork belongs to the heron species. Family! You'd think she was talking about people! The little, washed dung-beetle!

"Storks are never seen in this country. You'd see them on the Continent. In countries such as Denmark and Germany."

Finally they agreed to leave me at home. I'd be company for my uncle and be able to give him a hand.

Uncle Eoin was our favourite uncle of all. He'd give us sweets or a few coppers. He was a droll type of fellow, more level-headed than my father. My father often complained about him. He'd say he was a ne'er-do-well who was far too fond of the drink.

But my father was a severe man, very set in his ways. A glum sort, you'd rarely get a laugh out of him. He wasn't one for fun. He refused to take part in any kind of entertainment or let his hair down. Work is all he wanted, work, work and more work. He worked morning and night. On top of that, he was always pressing work on others.

He'd beat us, unlike Uncle Eoin. It seems like he spent most of his life battering one of us, or threatening us fiercely. He could be loutish with the neighbours too, finding faults with a lot of them. Above everything else he couldn't stand them drinking. He couldn't even put up with the mention of drink. I found this rather strange as I could remember him taking a drink himself, way back. And he could take a good few. He'd have a drink in the kitchen with the postman around Christmas. He'd down a few with cattle-buyers, duck-buyers and others. I remember the bottles and the empty glasses on the table, my father and his companion in jolly spirits. I used to knock back the dregs after them. But one night there was woeful ructions between my father and my mother. My mother was crying. We started crying too. Maybe that was what put an end to the boozing.

From that day on my father was morose, I thought. He spent his time slaving away, as though instructed by God. He improved his land beyond recognition (fresh green grass where once the heather wafted; rocks blown sky high and the neatest walls erected) so that his plot was the most noteworthy in the district.

I had done my share of labouring on the land and, even though I was only a young lad, I had asked myself over and over again what was it for. Why the endless slaving, why the seriousness of it all? Only rarely were we allowed to play hurling or football with our friends. We weren't allowed go to the circus or to the cinema. They were only a waste of time and money according to my father, suited only to those who would never make advancement in life. But he had plans for us that would ensure a bright future.

But Uncle Eoin was different, he was nice. He knew how to laugh. It was a wondrous, hearty laugh. Any time he'd be with us, he'd be out at night playing cards or up to some fun, instead of being chained to some chore at home. I'd see him taking the road to the village, a cap on his head, wearing a heavy brown coat, happy and content in himself, myself and my father in a state of half-collapse, feeding the calves and the cattle, up to the oxters in mud.

My uncle wasn't too particular what he wore. My father, though, wore a top hat for years, suits of the best tweed, and solid, leather shoes. For one reason or another my father was more respected than my uncle. People were a bit in awe of him – a straight, tough man – but somehow they respected him. They always spoke highly of him. My uncle was "a nice old sort" but my father was "a great man". How come? Why was that, I wonder? Because my father was married, with offspring to care for? My uncle hadn't chick or child or anything else. Was there more to it than that?

It was quite dark by the time Uncle Eoin and myself set out on the road. Not that it was all that late but it was that time of the year when night is in a hurry to fall.

During the evening, stars were beginning to bead the heavens and by now they were much clearer. Though a number of clouds sulked on high and the moon was covered, there were plenty enough omens to suggest a cold bright night ahead.

We were well wrapped: heavy coats and sturdy shoes. Uncle Eoin had his usual brown coat and his old cap. My head was bare. I didn't mind a bit though the cold wind was biting into my ears. I was so keen for this adventure that I'd walk to the North Pole in the nude. I ambled along, my hands in my pockets, and my heart was with me.

We took the main road. We could have shortened our journey

through the mountain paths but they were not to be trusted with their bog-holes, their quaking sods and marshland along the way. It was a route I had no knowledge of, except to view from Crew Hill, and it was a long time since Uncle Eoin himself tried it. The road was easier, if a little longer, and my uncle enjoyed walking at night.

And so we had to pass through the village. It wasn't the barracks that Uncle Eoin was worried about but fear of being recognized, of being drawn into conversation and forced to go for a drink.

He turned up the collar of his coat and we went dourly on without saying a word, but my heart was pounding with the spirit of adventure.

Ignoring the cold, the odd person stood outside the pubs. Not standing really: slouching against the wall or a lamp-post. In one pub a man was singing his lungs out, his voice rising with emotion.

By a dark gable a man was urinating.

At the other end of the village where the lights no longer reached us, my uncle gave me a shilling and I ran back to buy some sweets. He crouched behind a wall and you wouldn't see a speck of him.

I recognized the man who was pissing – it was Maidhc Learaí from Leegaun. A notorious drunk who spent his life with his lips to the glass, his house and land gone the way his piss was going now. And when I came out it was still streaming from him. It sounded so much like a cascade I wondered had he turned on a tap or something but as the thin, foam-topped channel appeared on the road, I knew it was pure piss. Like what might come out of a cow, except thinner.

As I went by, the pub door opened and I stole a quick glance inside where a fair few people were drinking. In front of them, on the counter, paraded pint-glasses with their fill of stout, some not so full. Big, tough, bare-chested men with caps, half-veiled by pipe and cigarette smoke. It was all so leisurely and so manly.

I was struck by a desire. To be in there among the men. I wanted to be grown-up and accepted in their company; to drink as good as the best of them. But my father! God save us! Quite mad he was. If he knew my mind he'd be horrified. He'd have a fit even if he saw me peering through the pub door – the door to the devil's kingdom! What sort was he at all that he had to be different from all living men?

Strange, but the police barracks is way back the other end, cut off from the town. As we passed it by, how proud I was of my uncle: off in search of illicit spirits and strolling innocently past the barracks. It was an expedition – a great adventure. We were play-acting – it was a show. My uncle was a fearless leader, as bold and as mischievous as the poteen-maker himself, Danann Mharcais, up to his alchemy as always in the wild hills beyond.

If the guards saw us they might get suspicious, I thought. We might be flung into prison. In my own mind I saw the "black hole" of the barracks, the firm, iron bolts on the closed door, rats whining in corners. We took a left turn: a sandy, narrow, crooked boreen winding its way through hedges and stones and out into the great open moorland. We passed the occasional house, an eerie pale-yellow light in some of the windows.

Soon we had reached a good height and the view to go with it. There were little torch-like lights to be seen a-plenty. The moon came out from a cloud and bathed the countryside in golden peace. In spite of the chill, and you'd notice the wind this high up, my heart was pumping with joy. I said to myself that the place was fierce lonesome and isolated and it pleased me to say it. Since an early age, the mountain and moor had a great attraction for me. I liked the bog-cotton and loved the heather. No bird was more delightful to me that the grouse.

My uncle took a leak and I commenced to do the same. It was a manly thing, I thought, to urinate with an adult. But I had soon finished and my Uncle Eoin's fine steady stream made me envious. His stream traced a circle around a patch of ice.

"That's your bog over there where the light is shining," said he, closing the buttons of his trousers and hoisting them up to his waist.

What he said interested me greatly. I looked eastwards towards the light and for a fraction of a second imagined myself there in the bog, spreading turf. My brother Cairbre beside me, my father below in the bog, cutting the turf and throwing up the sods. There were many places to be seen from that bog: hills that we could name, houses whose inhabitants were familiar to us, but it was towards Tamhnachaí Arda that my heart was ever drawn. There were stretches of land up there

that I had never laid eyes on, like many another. And somewhere there
. . . lived Danann Mharcais – the most renowned moonshiner in the
parish. Young and all as I was, I'd heard about this man and I always
imagined his children as moorchicks picking their way to school,
church or shops, through the heath.

Tamhnachaí Arda was a "land of youth" for me: it was there –
somewhere – and had always been there, old as time itself. The russet
hills all round, decayed mountain grass, Danann Mharcais ensconced
in his trench, concocting his potions. His father before him in the same
spot, or some other, and his father before him again, dedicated to the
same art. Watched by foxes unbeknownst. Wild birds scattering . . .

When we worked on the bog I'd ask my father about Danann. I'd
ask him all about Tamhnachaí Arda; and about poteen. But my father
didn't welcome such enquiries. "It's not poteen he makes but poison,"
he said one day, visibly angry, and told me to busy myself with the turf
and refrain from foolish chit-chat.

My father thought I was taking too much of an interest in Danann
Mharcais – the old man of the mountain, in his eyes, who never did
anything for himself or his family, only always causing trouble and
bother.

"He makes his devilish potion in a pig-trough, pisses and spits into
it, and then washes his feet in it."

He paused. He was upset. It wasn't right for me to be curious about
Danann. Not a healthy interest for a young boy at all at all!

"Danann and his kin are nothing but beggars, and self-respecting
people should give them a wide berth. They never had anything, famous
only for litigations and debts."

This was indeed an ugly portrait and it disgusted me sometimes;
but other times I'd be impressed by Danann's roguery and uncouthness.
I loved this distiller too much to take any notice of my father's prejudiced
outbursts. Many a person had a good word for Danann. My father was
a grouch.

And if Danann was in trouble with the law, it was the fault of the
law. Good man Danann! Guards in their stiff uniforms out on the side

of the mountain, waiting in ambush for Danann. The actions of those sneaking people drove me mad. Swooping down suddenly on the bold Danann's still, rendering it to pieces. What a blot on their souls.

"Do people put bluestone in the poteen?" I asked my uncle, unexpectedly.

"Some of them do," said he.

We came to a long lake, low-set between the brow of two hills. What a sight it was, the moon burnishing the surface. My heart took a joyful jump. This place was different – how different from where I lived along the road. A lake full of fish to be sure. And they'd be leaping on a fine summer's day . . .

Then suddenly we saw a white horse coming towards us from the lake. He moved slowly, awkwardly, in our direction.

"Would you look at that," exclaimed my uncle, transfixed, "Danann's old stallion!" His face shone, beaming like a schoolboy. "The poor beast, he's older than the mist! He must be bordering on forty – if he's not more!"

The stallion stood a little distance away from us. He stared at us. A melancholy look, I thought.

"*Pre! Pre! Pre!*" called my uncle to him, extending a hand. The stallion raised his head and looked at us askance. Suspicion in his eyes.

My uncle approached him, but he shied away. He stopped again. He whinnied, and sniffed the bare ground. His white hair was rough and patchy.

"The poor beast! He was grey once. Danann used to bring him round in the old days with a rusty machine and they'd cut the hay for the neighbours."

It was clear that my uncle had great affection for this aged animal, overjoyed to see him still alive. It was a sweet reminder of his youth.

We continued in silence, not noticing the silence such were the thoughts awakened in us. The moon poured her milk on us and on the untameable beauty all round. Ice was forming on lakes.

"What do the guards do with the poteen when they confiscate it?"

"Keep it."

"And then what?"

"Drink it, what else?" said he.

He straightened his shoulders and stuck out his chest.

"There's more poteen in the barracks of Moycullen than you'll find in the whole of Ireland," said he good-humouredly. "But do you know what I was thinking? Isn't it a quare thing! If that stallion were a human being he'd be a hundred and twenty years old!"

Danann Mharcais was getting on in years. He was older looking than I thought he'd be. A chubby face, round as a ball, clean-shaven. You'd imagine a beard wouldn't suit. His complexion remarkably red. One eye-socket was closed: he lost an eye in a rumpus outside the dance-hall when he was a teenager. Apart from the missing eye, it was a trouble-free face. His hands the strongest part of him: the palms like shovels, the fists of a boxer. What damage they could cause! I loved those hands; the eye that was gone, their history.

Danann was there with his feet outstretched, hobnail boots and all. Like my uncle, he wore a cap. He'd adjust it every so often. My uncle was a great man for the talk when the humour was on him. His vocabulary was tremendous, he never lacked an idiom or an image and it was said that there wasn't a man in the country with better Irish; but Danann Mharcais was taciturn, yet whatever much he had to say seemed weighty. Ply him with talk and he'd become contemplative, the eye fixed to the ground. He'd reply in a few words, or maybe ask another question, suddenly fixing the other in a one-eyed stare.

I must admit I was surrounded in a haze of pleasure in the company of this hero. I felt slightly heroic myself: in the company of Danann Mharcais whom I adored more than any in the world, my master, my inspiration, my very being.

Danann's wife made us some tea and while we were supping it, he went out. He wasn't long gone, though. When he came back he had a big aluminium bucket in his right hand, like the ones they use to milk the cows. He placed it on the table. Across he goes to the room and brings back a load of empty bottles, putting them standing on the floor beside him. He lifted the bucket from the table and sat down, proceeding to fill the bottles.

"This poteen is of a rare excellence," he said nonchalantly.

My heart raced. It was poteen in the bucket. God almighty! I was delighted and surprised he'd do this kind of work in my presence, but his daughter – who was even smaller than me – was also present.

The liquid running into the bottle could have been, for all the world, pure spring water. Though I'd often heard it was as colourless as water I never expected it to be so transparent.

"He never washed his feet in this stuff anyway," says I to myself, thinking about my father's remarks and wondering what truth they contained.

"Good stuff this I'm tellin' you," says Danann again, putting a cork in the bottle. "See the bubbles on top? Good sign!"

He went on filling until six bottles were full. When he had a cork on every bottle he rolled them up in old newspapers – as my mother would do with eggs for the market – and placed them in Uncle Eoin's grocery bag.

"That's a fine drop I'm tellin' you," he said for the third time, pocketing the price.

"It was never any other way, long life to you," said my uncle, gently.

"That stuff's even better still," says Danann.

There was still a drop left in the bucket and Danann poured two hefty scoops. He added some sugar and a quantity of boiling water.

"I prefer it as a punch," says Danann.

They took a swig.

"It's good with butter in it too – a knob of butter," said my uncle.

"Upon my soul it is and with buttermilk too," said Danann.

As they were about to have a second glass, Danann looked secretly, inquisitively, at my uncle and said, hardly audible:

"Maybe the young man here might like a drop?"

My uncle said nothing, pursing his lips in thought.

"It'll do him good, the night is cold," said Danann.

He looked at me askew.

"Will you have a drop of poteen – to wet your whistle?"

My heart churned because I knew well what they'd been saying. I was hardly able to open my mouth but I managed all the same.

"I will!" says I.

"Good lad," says Danann.

I felt the liquid burning me, but I was over the moon. I'd be tipsy to be sure but I didn't mind. The sweat came to my brow. Poteen! I was drinking poteen! Who'd believe it? Hard to believe! Me, in Danann Mharcais's house, drinking poteen. I'm going to be as drunk as a lord, am I? Would I be as bad as Maidhc Learaí? Would I be out pissing on the road – a long, straggling piss?

What would my father say if he heard of this? He'd kill me. He'd kill Uncle Eoin too. As sure as God he'd murder us. He'd go out of his skull with rage.

*   *   *

"A pity you drank that poteen," said Uncle Eoin as we walked down home. It was the last thing in the world I expected to hear. I was amazed. Why was he talking like that?

But I forget about it as a snipe rose suddenly from a stream on the side of the boreen. She darted angrily from her nest and commenced to cry. The urgent whirr of wings. No shortage of snipe here, I thought, what with all the water-holes unfrozen. I should bring my trap . . .

"A wee drop, I suppose it's no harm, but don't do it again," said my uncle, worriedly, as though there had been no break in conversation.

But this wasn't my uncle. This was my father talking. My uncle would have relished the mischief of it.

I sensed a barrier between us; a stone wall being built. My uncle had grown solemn and with the solemnity came tension. Something was weighing him down: that I had drunk poteen? But wasn't he the cause of it? A terror gripped me.

"I want to tell you something now but keep it to yourself – your father's an alcoholic."

The terror that gripped me was now taking hold. The exuberance in my soul died. It was not so much what he said as the way he had changed.

"Do you know what 'an alcoholic' is?"

"I don't."

"A drunk."

I thought about that a while. My father a drunk! The likes of Maidhc Learaí! A long, straggling piss? Taking two sides of the road coming home from the village!

"Respect your father," said my uncle, interrupting the flow of my thoughts. "He has a hard life, be of assistance to him!"

I was perplexed; my mind clouded over. We'd be home soon and the sooner the better.

"I'll hide these now before I head off in the morning. And, as I said to you before, say nothing to nobody about anything. Good boy!"

My uncle left the bag with the bottles behind the stone wall in a clump of briers a short distance from the house.

The following morning I woke up early. Something was telling me to steal the bottles. I looked out the window but it was hardly dawn yet.

I lay back in the bed again. No sooner had I done that but I was up again. If I stayed in bed any longer my uncle would be up and away.

I got out and put on my trousers and my shoes. I opened the bedroom door like a thief in the night, more stealthily than I knew was in me. It wasn't I that was going off to steal but another inside me. This wasn't me being wary but that same other within.

Hardly knowing what I was up to, oblivious to the cold and pookas, I scurried around the house, avoiding the window of the room in which my uncle was sleeping. I ran like the bejaysus, no stopping me: one goal goading me on and on. Little did I think that myself would be the thief when I warned my uncle last night to hide the bag in a safer spot, I said to myself. But that thief was not me but another inside me.

The bag was cold and semi-congealed. I snapped it out of the briers but as soon as I had possession of it I flipped. What would I do with it? Where would I put it? I stood in the middle of the garden, without any cover, like an undecided hare. I scurried across the garden. "I'll be caught," I said to myself, "If they catch me what will I do?" I looked around for cover. Put the bag back in the briers.

But maybe my uncle was watching? Better maybe to stay away from the house. Back down the garden again, further this time. Maybe someone was watching! Maybe there was someone behind the stone wall waiting for my next move.

I was sweating. I was confused. If I was being watched I'd be thought a lunatic. A complete whacko – running up and down the garden before the crack of day. They'd send me to Ballinasloe. I let the bag slip out of my hand where I stood and disappeared back into the house like a ghost.

I crept quietly through the house and back into bed. O hell, O blackest, blackest hell . . .

translated by Gabriel Rosenstock

PURPLE PLUMS

On a small island in Lough Corrib near Oughterard – an island called Inis na Bó or Cow Island – lived a family who worked for a bigwig. They were the Barretts and Barrett himself guarded the estate and was in charge of maintenance. They had their own little lodge behind the big house and a rowing-boat; strictly speaking they owned neither. The master never spent a winter there and was absent for long stretches of the year but the Barretts, like ordinary folk, eked out their daily existence on the island, looking after everything, the house, the land, the cattle. Like many before and since, they were often hard-pressed and it's said that the winters were bad in those days, so severe in fact that at times they'd be cut off from the rest of the world. One particular time they nearly starved to death. And then a white cow came out of the lake and gave them of her milk.

They might have been poor but it's said they were the best of company. They had a daughter, Bláthnaid, and they say she never stopped singing. As soon as she was of age, her responsibility was to help her mother with the flowers, the flowers of the big house, and help her father with the fowl, and whatever else the island lacked it had no scarcity of birds and botanic species because the squire was a collector and his beds boasted a great variety of flower and shrub. Thickets and stunted forest growth abounded with the strangest trees and bushes scattered all over the edge of the island; and the fowl were no less strange, peafowl, guinea-fowl and pheasants.

The Barretts would moor their boat in the tiny harbour of Barr-Roisín. You'd see them coming in, the father rowing, a hat on him, a suit of grey homespun cloth, a pipe in his mouth, puffing away. A big bony man. His wife was a shy type, a grey shawl on her head, sitting quietly at the back of the boat, facing the land. Their daughter was their pride and joy. She was spirited but well-mannered, verses and snatches of songs constantly on her lips. She'd be in the front, a ribbon in her hair, gaily dressed. When she was big enough she could ferry herself to the mainland, her pleasant voice reaching across the waters.

*   *   *

The time came for Bláthnaid to marry, another Barrett, from Moycullen, and they settled down in Uggool. Their little holding in Uggool was on top of a hill with a grand view over the glen. The glen was wooded and they could see far beyond, above the trees, to Lough Corrib. From this vantage point she could see the lake more clearly than ever before, most of it, from the Oughterard district to the city of Galway. The lake of lore, dotted with islands. An island for every day in the year, it was said.

She tried to count them but it seemed that some of them had merged. She used to study the horizon for Inis na Bó, Inse Ghaill and Oileán na gCloch, but they were too far away.

She'd see the boats and be struck with longing. As she went about her chores outside, she'd pause and watch the boats. She'd stand there or walk out to the potato patch. The boats that interested her were the ones going east in the morning and returning at evening. Who was on board and what was their business in Galway? She had no interest in those who were just out for the lake air. On Sundays she'd sit on a rock on the top of the hill and spend a long while watching.

The house she was in now was thatched, like the one she left behind on the island. Except this one was bigger and it was hers. Herself and her husband. A new thatch of yellow straw was put on for the wedding feast and the walls newly whitewashed. Two rooms separated by a spacious kitchen. The front door right in the middle of the house and the closed back-door behind. The doors were newly painted and the window-frames.

It was a fine big kitchen. The hearth was generous. Plenty hooks on the crane. There were piglets and calves to fatten.

Opposite the fire, its back to the wall, stood a large dresser that doubled up as a press. Shelves bulging with crockery. Plates standing. The big plates on the upper shelf. Hooks attached to the shelves on which cups hung. Jugs on the lower shelf.

A hob on each side of the fireplace. Turf and blocks of wood in the nook. It was said that Peadar, her husband, was as good as any man in the parish with a turf-spade or an axe.

Bláthnaid fitted out the house in her own style. It was she who picked the curtains for the windows, the table, the chairs. It was she furnished the rooms.

The ground in front of the house was swept and fresh sand scattered along its length. Peadar built a stone wall in front with beds of clay beside it. When she visited home, Bláthnaid would bring back bulbs, roots and flower seeds and cuttings from flowering trees. Exotic trees. Exotic plants. Before long there was hardly a flower, tree or plant on the island that hadn't been duplicated in Uggool by Bláthnaid.

When her husband brought a turf-cart to Galway or a load of potatoes, Bláthnaid had her own share of flowers and vegetables for the market. And as for fowl, she wanted to have birds as well. Grey geese, ducks and hens.

Sometimes Bláthnaid would take a stroll on the moor behind the house, from where she had the best view of the lake to the north. But that was not why she liked to stroll there but to collect her thoughts, reflect on her life. The life that was, the life that is. Her future.

But her mind would stray to other things as well. A reclusive flower. A well-built stone wall or a mound her husband had just made. Many is the time she watched the birds. Birds of the moor. Peewits and plovers. The golden plover was great company and had a pleasant song. And when her mind turned to this song or when she'd hear the curlews, all black thoughts would flee her.

When curlews rose in flight and started their cry, her heart, too, would rise. She would pause and look at them in the sky, knowing they would plummet again soon and sometimes she'd move to where they were. Rising again plaintively in one flock, as rowdy as a crowd of children. Children!

One day the bigwig from the island visited Uggool unexpectedly and brought a present for them. It was no ordinary present. Nor was it an ordinary pheasant from the woods but a golden hen-pheasant. She was in a cage in his carriage. It was the most beautiful bird that Bláthnaid had ever seen and she wept.

"Well, well, well!"

"This will bring you luck!"

*   *   *

The boreen to Uggool takes you through the townland of Kylebroughlaun. Another couple lived at the mouth of the road with whom they shared the same surname; they had a child, a youngster with a speech impediment and Bláthnaid was his godmother. Since he was very young, the boy was accustomed to look out for the Barretts on Saturday evenings as they returned from Galway in their horse and cart. Having deposited their load in the big town, the Barretts – Bláthnaid and Peadar – would be seated up front on a pink, wooden board. The boy would recognize the sound of the cart coming up the road. Whether walking or trotting, he'd know the clatter of the horseshoes. He'd stand a bit up the boreen, away from the mouth of the road, half shyly, half boldly. Bláthnaid's shawl no longer on her head, covering her shoulders. She would be expecting him.

The boy would often visit Uggool, crossing over the gardens. He'd give Peadar a hand. He'd help Bláthnaid as well. He'd bring the piglets their feed and the calves too, muzzling them or using cow-dung so they wouldn't be sucking one another.

He'd look after the children, bringing them to the woods nearby to play, hunting or playing hide-and-seek. They'd be brought to the house and given bread and jam. One day the boy was given a present out of the blue – not a biscuit from a box or a sweet from a bag. A duck! A duck with the oddest colours. Black and white. The wings and the tail were black. But the red crest on the head, around the eyes, that was the most peculiar thing of all.

Bláthnaid tied the legs with strips of cloth and put it into a bag – the body – and secured the bag with string. The boy took off with his package over the gardens, the long neck of the duck outstretched; the beak and the eyes.

"Well, well, well!"

*   *   *

Bláthnaid Barrett is still alive. She still lives in her house in Uggool, one of her sons, his wife and their children under the same roof. The boy himself is married and lives in Kylebroughlaun. Bláthnaid is the oldest person in the region. She says she's had a good, hard life.

translated by Gabriel Rosenstock

A FATEFUL DAY

Seeing that I hadn't done my lessons the evening before or in the morning either I hadn't noticed that my school-bag was missing until I came in from setting snares, and by then it was past time for me to have left for school. Now, in a great hurry, and up in a heap, I frantically searched for it. The awful thing was that the inspector was to be in the school that day and, anyway, Mrs McSurly, the schoolmistress, was always very cross with anyone who was late.

I threatened to stay at home, all my brothers and sisters having gone for ages, but my mother wouldn't hear of it.

"Off with you, now, bag or no bag!" she said, she in a fit that I went out into the gardens unbeknownst to her; she having given me new socks and new sandals for the big occasion.

I said that she was to blame for my bag because I had left it on the table, and that I wouldn't go to school without it. But I did. I set off peevishly and I felt very odd: each hand as long as the other and nothing in them.

I walked slowly at first, pretending that I didn't give a damn, but it wasn't long before I began to run. There was a new surface on the boreen, it was rough and it was hard to run or walk on it with any comfort. As well as that I was complaining madly to myself at not having done my lessons, especially seeing that I had told myself firmly that I would do them in the morning.

I recalled times before when I was in a fix but this was the biggest fix yet. The phrase "no matter how long the fox escapes he is caught in the end" kept coming into my head and I felt that this was the time, surely, that I'd be caught.

I started to run again but suddenly I hit the top of my sandal against a stone on the road and a bit of the sole tore off. I also hurt my big toe.

"Blast it!" I said.

I considered hiding in the mountain.

Another thought struck me, however: I'd pick a bunch of flowers for the teacher and maybe, then, she wouldn't be too hard on me. Immediately,

I was very taken by this idea and a great hope ran through me. On many mornings girls brought flowers – daffodils, crocuses and other types of flowers – and the teacher put them in jamjars on the window-sill.

I went into the mountain and I pulled some orchids and other flowers, blue ones and yellow ones, that I didn't know their names; pulling them as deep down as I could so that the shanks would be as long as possible.

Coming near the school, however, my enthusiasm started to wane. Down on the plain I felt ridiculous. I was thinking that my flowers weren't flowers at all, only weeds. I thought about throwing them away, but for some reason I held on to them. It was a great relief, at any rate, to see that there wasn't any strange car outside the school.

The teacher took my present and immediately threw the flowers into the rubbish-bin. She grabbed me by the hair and shook my head backwards and forwards. From the drawer of her table she took out one of her sticks, the hazel-rod, and gave me two slaps.

"What's the use talking to you?" she said.

But she didn't notice that I hadn't my school-bag and that was the main thing.

Down I went to my old place at the back of the class. I wasn't much upset. The slaps didn't bother me a bit, and as for her throwing the flowers in the bin it was more or less what I expected: that they weren't flowers at all even if they looked nice. If flowers grew that easily who would be without them?

As I sat there, looking sideways into my companion's book, I didn't feel bad at all. I felt safe. I was sweating but that was no bother. I felt great that so much of my worry was over.

I startled again, however, when Mionla McKinane was asked to teach the class. Mrs McSurly did this sometimes but it was an exercise that I didn't like. Although Mionla was far easier than Mrs McSurly I resented her. She was only one of the class herself and I always felt humiliated when she acted as teacher.

She was an engineer's daughter, new to the parish. They lived in a big house with lots of strange shrubbery around it, near enough to us, and they had a motor car.

My father liked them, he said that they were kind people and that there wasn't a bad thing about them, that they were good neighbours and all. Sometimes he would send milk to their house for good turns they had done, like lifts to town in the car. But I couldn't like them. I would never forget the time that Mr McKinane had said, in Mionla's presence, that there were potato-skins in the milk; she picking out a little bit of boiled skin as proof.

I didn't like their company at all, because they were much richer than we were and they were far better dressed. Mionla's clothes were far prettier than the clothes worn by my sisters. And, at this time, they were negotiating with my father to buy our garden by the river. They were adamant about it and my father kept saying that he needed the money.

At the teacher's advice Mionla put us doing dictation and this was the devil altogether. I hated dictation.

For me dictation equated with the teacher's thorny blackthorn stick on the top of my head. I was that bad at spelling.

However, Mionla was scarcely in charge of us when Mrs McSurly stopped her again. She took charge of us herself. In no time at all a knock came on the door, a gentle knock, and the door opened wide. A big tall man walked in. He wore a fine suit and carried a big leather bag in his hand.

He spoke kindly to Mrs McSurly and he shook hands with her. We stood and then we sat. The word "inspector" was beating loudly, like a clock, in each of our hearts.

After a short conversation with the teacher the man sat down at the table and he started to write with a fountain-pen in his notebook.

Everyone was well-mannered. Mrs McSurly was never as nice but we could see a glint in her eye that told us that this was the big moment; that anyone who failed would be in trouble, that he would lose the grant and that, maybe, he would be expelled from school for ever.

When the inspector rose from the table and when he came over to us all our hearts started to beat violently. We were full of nerves. None the less I couldn't but notice his physique. He was a fine man. Standing there before us he even looked bigger than when he first came in. He had a grand head of hair and it was nicely combed. His shoes shone. His trousers were finely creased. It was the best-creased trousers that I had ever seen. The crease on each leg, front and back, as sharp as a knife.

He greeted us in a very kind way but, nevertheless, his strangeness frightened us. Only that I was preoccupied with the creases in his trousers I'd be shaking with fear. They were, surely, the most noticeable creases that I had ever laid eyes on.

Suddenly Tadhg was called up and he was quietly told to go to the shop for a sweet cake, and to fetch a can of water from the well on his way back.

For whatever reason Tadhg was the teacher's pet. It was he who was asked to do every message. I resented this, because Tadhg was my younger brother; although, by this time, I was getting used to it. We were in the one class and the teacher used often annoy me by saying: "Why can't you be a little more like your young brother?"

Today, at any rate, I regretted whatever misdemeanour she had seen in me because if I was Tadhg, maybe, then, it would be me who would be free at this time.

I heard the crows calling in the big trees in the Nursery at the side of the school as if scolding someone for having disturbed them. That was Tadhg. Wasn't Tadhg the lucky fellow? It would be lovely to be free, standing at the bottom of the trees looking up at the crows. This was a pastime that I really liked. I would spend lots of time looking up at them, flying from tree to tree, from branch to branch, making their loud commotion.

I loved their raucous noise. I loved their clamour. Their noisy bedlam was most pleasant to my ear. "Caw! Caw! Caw!" It was one of the nicest bird-noises. Fresh! It seemed to gush forth. Vibrant! Dawn! Dew! Daybreak! It was the epitome of freedom.

A pang of sadness came over me. I wished I had my school-bag. I wished I had my own book in front of me. It would be ages before it was three o'clock. But we'd have a break for lunch.

That wasn't much good. What was a break like that compared to Tadhg's freedom? Lunch-break was an ordinary break, everyone was free, but the freedom given to Tadhg was special. It was like being lucky or wise. That freedom was much nicer.

The teacher started to prepare some tea for the inspector. She boiled the water in a kettle on the small stove and wet the tea, and she cut the sweet cake into slices.

I watched her cut the cake. I inspected the slices. She cut the slices into halves.

The cake was browner outside than inside. Outside it was the colour of honey. Delicious, I thought to myself. My mouth desired a bit. If only I could eat a half-slice!

An inspector's cake, I said to myself. I thought that it must have been made especially for an inspector because I had never before seen a cake like it. What a beautiful cake!

If I was an inspector I'd be eating cakes like that. I'd be eating heaps of cakes. Cut nicely like this one.

I might be an inspector. Then, I'd be dressed like a gentleman. I'd have a leather bag in my hand and I'd have shiny creases in my trousers. And I'd be gorging sweet cake in every school.

A piece of paper was sent from person to person to me: telling me that I had caught a hare in a snare. Alive! Tadhg was told the news in the village. My father had taken him in and he was being kept tied in my bedroom until I came home.

The whole class was excited. Everyone was looking back at me. I was delighted. Absolutely thrilled. I found it hard to believe. Which ever snare it was? Hares rarely got caught in snares. It must be one of the three I had set in the mountain, I thought. Brilliant! A hare was much better than a rabbit.

I envisaged the hare in my mind: out in the mountain, long ears, listening attentively, looking about him. Running off a short distance, stopping and sitting back. Sitting back on his bottom. Stretching himself upwards, listening and looking. His short front paws as if ready to go boxing.

A red hare! Of good appearance! His fur showing the sign of full health and vigour. Because of his shorter front paws a hare could run faster uphill than downhill. Downhill he would topple over if going too fast.

I didn't fear the inspector any more. Nor did I fear Mrs McSurly. The inspector could ask me any question he liked. She could beat me all she liked. Neither of them had a hare, and it was unlikely that they ever would have one. But I had. In my bedroom.

The way the inspector was going it was unlikely that he'd get as far as me before lunch-break. But, of course, there was always a fear that he would. Because he didn't assiduously follow any order. That was the trouble.

Every time, however, that I felt in danger all I did was to remember my hare at home and I was immediately filled with renewed confidence. To such a degree that I could endure any pain, insult or slap.

By lunch-time I regretted that I hadn't been examined. I'd be finished, then. But, anyway, my hare was at home waiting for me.

After lunch it appeared that the inspector was hurrying. He was rapidly closing in on me. I felt as if I was being trapped in an ever-shrinking patch of ground. I was calling on my hare but somehow his presence didn't appear to possess the same magical power as before. He, too, was frightened. I felt like the hare myself. I kept my head down.

When the inspector came to my turn I was almost stuck to the seat; like an ostrich hoping against hope not to be seen. Even my eyelashes scarcely moved. Although my body stayed rigid my brain prayed. I prayed most fervently, requesting and beseeching, that in some strange way I might be missed.

I wasn't. I was caught. I raised myself in a stooped position and I felt more exposed than I ever felt in my life. My shape was often silhouetted against the sky as I walked the windy mountain boreen but that was no exposure compared to this. Every eye staring at me. I madly desired to escape, to run away. To be again on that lonely windy boreen. What a freedom that would be compared to this hot humiliating prison.

Although I was considered a big strong lad, full of energy and strength if I was itself, my knees were knocking together. I was almost pissing in my pants with fright, seeing all those faces making fun of me.

At first when the inspector called my name I managed a kind of smile, a wry distorted smile, but in no time at all I was fecked; I couldn't smile or answer, although he was nice and pleasant. All I wanted was to be quickly put out of my misery. That he would see at once that I wasn't capable of answering any question that he might ask me.

Suddenly Mrs McSurly whispered something to him.

"He's from Tawnaghalougha!" I heard her say.

For some reason or other the inspector thought that significant. He immediately took a new interest in me. He turned his book to me and he asked:

"What animal is that?"

"A hare!" I said.

"Say that in Irish!" he said.

"*Giorria!*" I said.

"'*Giorr-i-a!*'" he repeated after me and he wrote it like that on the blackboard. Then he got the whole class to repeat it as I had said it.

"Where does a hare sleep?" he asked.

"In a red bed!" I answered.

"'In a red bed!'" he repeated. "*I leaba dhearg!*"

We talked some more and I was dying to tell him about my hare at home, but I didn't.

Then he changed the subject.

"Are there fish in that lake up there?" he asked.

"There are!" I answered.

"What type of fish?" he asked.

"Salmon and white trout!" I answered.

"What do you call 'white trout' in Irish?" he asked.

"*Liatháin!*" I answered.

" '*Liatháin!*' " he said after me.

When he was finished he handed me sixpence and I was as happy as if I were in Heaven. I said to myself that I'd buy a yellow orange with the money and that I'd give it to the inspector. He'd give me another sixpence and I'd do likewise with it.

But that wasn't what I did. Instead I bought myself a bag of sweets.

On my way home, east of the village, I went to take a drink of water from the tap and suddenly I spotted my black school-bag on the green grass beside the wall. Immediately I remembered having left it there the evening before.

translated by the author

PRECIOUS MOMENTS

It was the morning of the day of the Twelfth-night.

In spite of the severe cold Mary Faherty rose early, as early as any other winter's morning. She was expecting to witness a heavy coat of snow on the ground because of the grey appearance of the sky the evening before; the odd snowflake falling when she was going to bed.

Standing in her bare feet she viewed the wide expanse of countryside from the small window of her bedroom. The day was only dawning. There was, indeed, a fine coat of snow outside.

Everywhere and everything, with the exception of the lake, was shrouded white. The bogs, the fens, the marshes – right up to the banks of the lake – they were all white. Just two colours to be seen: the white of the land and the grey of the lake and the sky.

The grey water didn't look healthy. It looked sick, like a huge trough of stagnant liquid. But that didn't bother Mary. The water was calm. Not a ripple on it. Unlike most other winter mornings there wasn't the slightest whisper of breeze, even from the west gable-end of the house.

The whiteness pleased her. Snow always pleased her. Ever since she was a child. Every winter she longed for snow. Not just a sprinkle of snow but a good, healthy, heavy, fall. Snow at Christmas-time, that was how God wanted it, she felt.

Snow transformed an area. Making it pure and beautiful. It brought a blessing with it, a joyful silence. Permitting one to talk at one's comfort with the Creator.

"Blessed be God most high!"

She raked out the live embers of the old fire and lit a new fire of turf: putting two sods lying on top of each other at the back, the embers in the middle, and a semicircle of standing clods by the perimeter.

She hung the kettle of water over the fire, and then she went on her knees on the floor, her elbows resting on the seat of a chair, her back to the fire, saying her prayers.

When she had eaten a bite, and swallowed a drop of tea, she would go out, "this blessed morning", and let out the dog and hens. There wouldn't be much for the hens to pick but they could scratch the snow and, anyway, she'd enjoy the harsh healthy air on her face; inhaling a few hefty draughts of it into her lungs.

Some blobs of snow fell down on her the moment she opened the door. Some wrens were flying about. Such tiny birds! But lovely. They had come out of the eaves of the thatch. She regretted that St Stephen's Day was over.

East of the house, at the bottom of the coniferous shelter-belt where there was still some uncovered earth, a blackbird and a robin foraged for food. The blackbird was a male, she knew that from its bright-yellow bill. How shiny bright! The robin sporting its red breast.

Mary's heart was full of joy. What pleasing contrasts: the jet-black blackbird, its bright-yellow bill; the robin's red breast, and the pure whiteness of the snow!

"Glory be to God!"

These were happy signs. Good omens. The robin accompanied Christ when he was crucified. Christ's blood fell on its breast. Her favourite Christmas cards displayed the robin on them.

She walked around the house, her wellington boots crunching the virgin snow, leaving their imprints. What a lovely white cover of snow that lay on the house-roof! So gentle and soft! Likewise, on top of the granite wall of the haggard.

The white contours of the countryside. The hills. The glens. "The Himalayas" beyond. Hehir's currachs. Everything.

Very little movement anywhere. Restfulness. Perhaps there were small animals out hunting but it would be hard to see them. Mice, rats, otters, they would leave their tracks.

The sheep had been gathered. They were housed. There weren't many sheep nowadays.

Curran's, Barrett's, Hehir's. And the Faherty's. These were all the houses that were left.

Curran's was the newest house. It was the only concrete house. But who was in it? Nobody. They left a couple of years after building it. All away, now, in foreign parts. The land leased to Colin Barrett.

The ruins of Martin Shéamais's house down below. He, another Barrett. His land gone to rack and ruin. He never left it to anybody, he never made a will. Bog-cotton growing where he used to have potatoes and turnips. He had a brother, Michael, in Ballinasloe, but he didn't own it. And what good would it be to him anyway? Not a sinner ever visiting him.

Bridie Hehir on the hill above to the south. Same age as herself. Her house in a very bad state. No way in but a path through the currachs. She had to come through her path to get that far. Never greeted. Hadn't greeted for ages. Pulled down her shawl over her head and never spoke, although they had gone to school together.

Bridie wore a long dress like she wore herself; down over the tops of her wellington boots.

Bridie's husband was long dead, like her own husband. Bridie had a son, Tom, in England but he rarely came home, or wrote. Her own daughter, Mary, died of TB. A beautiful girl. She was only twelve.

A few old folk, now, that was all that was left in the whole village of Tullagh. Tullaghalougha! The "remnants of the tribe" as someone had put it.

Now, it was all up to Colin Barrett. And he wasn't young either. It was very doubtful, at his age, that he'd ever get married. Who would marry him? Still and all somebody might, there was always someone, if only he searched properly.

It was unlikely, either, that Tom Hehir would ever return. What for, really? Although if he was any good he could do many the thing. A real harum-scarum. The Hehirs would die out like the Faherties.

But the Faherty blood was still there. If only just. She would have to mind herself.

"God between us and all harm!"

She heard a hen call. Announcing that she had laid an egg. A fine call. A hearty call. A proud call. A call as arrogant as any hen. Why not? It warmed Mary's spirits.

She thought about the call. A triumphant call. Full of courage and hope.

A young call. Brave and innocent like the bleat of a lamb. As safe and satisfied as the laugh of a bold child.

This was the wholesome sound of a haggard. The joyful cry of an expectant dawn.

Two dark-brown hen-eggs tucked tightly under a thick clump of red ferns. The ferns capped with snow. The nest-egg and the newly-laid egg. They were the pretty sight in the cosy comfort of the nest!

How pleasing it was to have a hen lay when most hens were in their non-laying season!

She stood looking in at the nest. The sight of fresh eggs snug in their nest was always something to behold. Especially in a well-concealed nest.

No matter how often she had witnessed it, it always gladdened her heart. A birth. Each newly-laid egg was a new birth. These eggs so carefully, so skilfully, sheltered from the cold elements. So warm within, so bleak without.

She retrieved the old nest-egg, leaving the newly-laid one to do its duty.

The cock was proudly scratching the earth-floor of the old barn. Chuckling, cackling, gurgling. Warning. Digging. Observing. His tall red comb slightly swaying.

"God be with her people who had built that barn, who had worked the horse-cart, the iron plough and the harrow!"

There were so many old bits of machinery. All rusting and rotting.

She the last of the family. She had better mind herself. It was up to her to prolong the family name for a little while longer. But there was no point in getting too uptight about it. As of yet, at any rate, there was still Faherty blood in the townland of Tullaghalougha.

What would happen when she was gone? Who would buy her land? Faherty land!

The wheel would turn. But, alas, not for her family. It was happening already in some areas. People were now seeking out remote places. Monied people.

In the future sites, would be bought and houses would be built, fine big houses. Attractive houses, with prominent exaggerated windows. There would be motor cars, and garages to house them. But not for her folk.

"God bless the old people!"

What was sad was how the old stock would be forgotten and their memories discarded with them; after all they had done. All their toil and good work. Neglected, banished and forgotten. That was a pity.

She scanned the area to the north-east. Keagh and the hills of Letter. Down in the glen, behind those hills, lay the village. The village was on the main road. A by-road branched from the main road. Her road branched from the by-road. Just now all roads were covered with snow.

A stranger wouldn't know the roads with the snow. Wouldn't know there was a road. She would. She knew the contours; the brinks and the bushes.

The ruts and the crests were all levelled. The ruts of the donkey- and horse-carts; of the motor cars of the fishermen and the fowlers.

That night Mary lit the twelve candles, the same as she did every other Twelfth-night. Small candles of different colours: yellow, red, green and blue.

She lit them, as always, on the same timber-bar, a bar that also acted as a door-bar at night and as a bar for mashing boiled potatoes in the large pot. As always she put the bar lying on the kitchen table beside the window and put the candles standing on it. The window facing the road.

She was now the same age as her husband when he died. The same age as her father and her mother. None of her people were more long-lived now than she was, and they were all long-lived. Twelve years her senior her husband was when he died outside, weeding the turnips.

She counted the years since: eleven, ten, nine . . . one.

A flame from the fire on a piece of twisted paper that was how she brought light to the candles. An uncouth way, she had always thought, and she wished for a more sophisticated method because the lighting of the twelve candles required proficiency. What was needed was that all the candles be lit at the one time, or barring that, in quick sequence. One shouldn't much precede the other, nor should any wind or puff of air blow on one rather than on the other, because this was a race: a race of time and life. This was a test. A test of endurance and life-span. The first candle to quench, the person whose name was attached to it was the first to die.

Like every other year Mary attached a name, on a little slip of paper, to each candle. Her own name. The name of her husband, her daughter's name. The names of her brothers and sisters. Her father's name and that of her mother's. All of them now dead save herself.

Every year hers was the last candle to die, and she thought that strange. Her religion told her not to pay any heed to this but she believed it to be an omen.

She sat down by the fire to watch the candle-race as she had done every other Twelfth-night. It would take an hour or so. She loved the sight of the candles. All the colours. The black wicks. The yellow lights, at times flickering like angels dancing. Red, blue, yellow, green. A holy night. Almost as holy as Christmas night.

It was also a sad night. Christmas over for another year. One day to go: the Twelfth-day.

The stems were shortening. Sometimes the dam of candle-grease at the bottom of the burning-wick would burst and run down the side; hardening again, however, and leaving a decorative design.

As the candles wore on the battle became more intense. The souls of the candles struggled. Gasping for life. These were the precious last moments.

Lost in thought she stared into the distance. In her mind's eye she saw the white snow. The white-blanketed countryside. The snowflakes falling gently. White quietness to the ends of the earth. No stir, no movement. Serenity. Holiness.

There was a young woman, dressed in white, standing at the head of the road. Tall, slim, with well-shaped thighs and long hands. Fine dark hair down to her waist. Clothed in a flowing frock down to her heels.

There was a black-haired young man with her. Tall and handsome. Wearing a black suit and a high hat. He had doffed his hat and he was curtsying to the woman. She swinging to face him, her frock flowing like a cloak. He taking her hand. She staring him in the eyes, they both moving to kiss each other. Gently, lovingly, of one mind, oblivious to the world.

Mary felt tranquil. Peaceful, at ease, young and in love. Optimism flowed through her body. Bravely.

The young couple, hand in hand, were walking towards her. Sometimes they giddily hopped and skipped, but they weren't coming any closer. The woman on occasions reclined her head and allowed it to rest on the man's breast. How lovely! Their lives entwined. How lovely! Sun and snow shone. Birds and children sang.

Momentarily she was distracted by the candles. By now they were short and weak. Shortly they would begin to die. Some of them would fight, others would die quickly; a clean death without resistance.

Once again hers was the last candle. Its butt short and struggling. Its strength ebbing.

Its slender black wick standing alone in the middle of its small pool of watery grease. The wick fell but its flame did not extinguish. Its root continued to draw sustenance from the lubrication that surrounded it. Once more it blew into a wide white light.

When the fat wore thin, the flame caught hold of the timber and a small black stain appeared.

The sky had changed. Its sullen texture metamorphosed to brightness. It was freezing sharply. A galaxy of twinkling stars appeared in the heavens, shepherded by a diamond moon.

Purity. Holiness. Sacredness.

Mary sensed that eyes viewed her through the window. Although this sense came suddenly to her she did not startle, because the eyes did not come promptly but gently and slowly as if out of a fog.

The eyes were those of an old woman. Penetrating red-rimmed eyes. Very red. As red as blood. They looked without blinking through the glass-pane. Hoisted to the centre of the pane, staring. Staring at her. They had neither head nor body attached to them.

They were her grandmother's eyes, she recognized them. Sixty years ago. They were her mother's eyes. Thirty years ago. They were her own eyes.

She reclined her head. The numinous light of her candle took hold of the little strip of paper on which "Mary" was written. Once more the flame increased. Then, without clamour or shout, a light breath of cloud ascended.

translated by the author

DARA Ó CONAOLA

Born on Inis Meáin in the Aran Islands, but now living on the neighbouring island, Inis Oírr. Has written a number of books, including short stories, a novella, stories for children and local history. Many of his short stories have been translated into English and were published in the collection *Night Ructions*. Dara's fascinating and much-acclaimed writing is full of wonder and imagination.

Runs a craft shop and also teaches.

NIGHT RUCTIONS

It was night, almost. The boy was in a hurry. Didn't fancy being caught in the dark. But it wouldn't be all that black, he thought. Hadn't he been playing on the road the night before and all was bright as the living day.

Never mind that. He wouldn't like to be going down Barr 'n Fhána too late as it was an eerie spot.

"Sure, I'll throw in a couple of stones," he said as he built up the gap. "They'd never go over the two stones."

He meant the small flock of sheep and the big ram that were gathered in the middle of the mound and appeared to be happy enough with themselves. And why wouldn't they be?

They had plenty of grass. They wouldn't be there at all, of course, were it not so late and the boy not able to bring them out any further on the crags.

He threw a few stones in the gap as planned and hurried off.

The sheep stood immobile in the middle of the ground at first but bit by bit they began to graze.

Night spread over the island. The sky darkened at first but then began to grey, and night took on its own shape.

The moon or a sliver of moon was somewhere but was hidden by a frosty vapour that filled the entire sky. You couldn't say it was dark. Maybe, even, the moon was full somewhere, busily penetrating the film of hoar.

The spirit of night was activating all things around. Reminding the bird it was time to doze. It drove the boy home. Night's business is best left to the night.

The same spirit had got into the big ram. In this charged atmosphere he glimpsed the reason and the importance of his being. An inexplicable feeling coursed through his blood. He could feel an inborn strength beginning to manifest itself and sensed the dignity and power which is the stamp of sovereignty.

And who could dispute his rule? Not alone on this mound. Anywhere! Still, he kept himself in check.

Shaking himself vigorously he went off in search of some sweet grass.

The moon was somewhere.

By this time it was fully night. The peace which most earth creatures desire was palpable in the air.

But also coming to a head was that giddiness which night inspires in its more adventurous denizens.

The big ram was one of that minority which night calls to high-headed deeds.

Like all his kind, he got little opportunity to prove himself, confined as he was to his own domain.

But things would change tonight!

He looked at the few stones casually thrown in the gap by the boy – the only obstacle between him and the wide world. He could see how easily he might toss them aside.

This was the chance he had been waiting for.

Whenever this night-time fitfulness got hold of him nothing could satisfy him but to break loose.

Hemmed in feeling . . . What wouldn't he give to be out there and show the strutting high and mighty who was in charge.

Suddenly the stones were down.

Baa-a-a. The sheep startled and huddled together in the centre of the mound, seeing it was the big ram that had caused the furore.

They knew the big fellow was out for ructions. Nothing would stop him now.

On the road. Free. He could do anything he liked now, as nature prodded him.

The sheep followed. One after the other. Following him out on the road. Not knowing where they were going. He didn't quite know himself. But he was on his way.

He went out past the Old Milking Place. Stopped at Beartleen's Gap – nothing much there to rouse him. Out again.

It was still and you could hear his keen footfall coming through the eerie wisps of night. The sheep straggling behind.

Cló Naomh. Nothing stirring here. The procession continued.

They stopped at *Róidín na bPúcaí.* Momentarily between two minds. Down the boreen or stay on the road? Stay on the road. On. And on.

They passed *Crogán a' Cheannaigh. Creig na gCrúibíní. Róidín an Phríosúin. Buailtín a' tSagairt.* Towards *Macha – Macha Mór.* On to *Ceann an Bhóthair.*

There was more. Though the road stopped suddenly a great expanse lay beyond. Where the ditch crossing the road ended were two gaps. One to the right, the other to the left. A ditch separating the two gaps, dividing two mounds.

The big ram made for the east gap. The mound to the east.

It had sheep. Scattered here and there along the mound. Some lying down.

In among them the Young Ram. Proud as a king. He heard the commotion at the gap. A fit of pique. He recognized the Big Ram.

And the Big Ram recognized him. And he knew that it was this young ram that had made him frantic all night. He felt his blood seething, goading him on. He would face fiercely any foe that dared countenance him.

That challenge awaited him beyond the gap. Now that he was free and unfettered it would be so easy just to walk in.

The fellow inside was in fighting fettle too. He also wanted to assert his supremacy. He wanted to be free and display to the world what prowess he could command.

They faced one another. The Big Ram and the Young Ram. They didn't spend long sizing each other up. There was no holding them now. They were free to lash into the fray.

Crash! Two skulls collided. All a-tremble. The Young Ram more badly shaken. Lost his ground. The big fellow's next assault threw him even further back. It was clear that the Big Ram had more fire and wind.

The Young Ram backed off. Fell. Up again in a flash. Faced the Big Ram, again and again. Collapsing, again and again . . .

They moved to the outer edge of the mound. Through hollow and hillock. Over soft ground and stone. The Young Ram falling, retreating . . .

Until they came to the ditch outside. *The wall of Macha.* The Young Ram had no where else to go. But he wouldn't yield. He faced the Big Ram . . .

And the Big Ram faced him – standing on his two hind legs and pumping all his strength into every shape he made.

The Young Ram didn't know where he was, or in what world . . . The next onrush floored him completely.

All feet in the air. Tongue out. He had it. For good.

The Big Ram had done the deed. He turned back. But, trying to walk, the legs buckled under him. On his knees. Attempting to rise he crashed over on his side.

A little glen behind him. He rolled down on his side. Couldn't get up.

For a while his legs were twisting and turning like a dog having a dream. Then the legs stiffened and the Big Ram lay motionless – not a twitch.

The sky had brightened. The frost of earlier was on the run and the moonlight streamed through.

Nightclouds moved silently, peacefully. The sky smiled. The Goddess of the night smiled . . .

Satisfied, it would seem.

translated by Gabriel Rosenstock

SORELY PRESSED

It was the great Daniel O'Connell himself who caused me my misfortune – well-beloved and all as he was by the Irish race. Sure they thought he was the Almighty. I had great praise for him myself. I'd work for him for nothing. I would – until that night.

"Where was I again?"

"You were in the big city, of course."

"That much I know – but where?"

"You were in that pub you're always in. Didn't you spend the day there?"

"Where did I go after that?"

"You said, eventually, that you were heading off. Nothing would keep you. You vamoosed. That's all I remember . . ."

I suppose since we can't recall, I'll never find out for sure where I went. I must have been in a few places and whiled away the time somewhere. I've never heard of a couple of hours that went missing in this life without someone using them up. I suppose I came by Trinity College. Down then towards the bridge they call O'Connell Bridge. The bridge of Danieleen of the Gaelic. Wasn't it the Gaelic saved him! "Daniel O'Connell, have you Irish in your head?" said the maid from Ireland to him, in the old tongue. "What's on your mind, let it be said," said Daniel, not thinking of anything in particular, no more than I was that night. "Ah," says she, "there's poison in your cup to kill you stone-dead." It's a long time now since I heard that tale from Darky John. "It was, you know," said Darky, "it was the Gaelic what saved him . . ." And may God rest Darky John, Daniel, the maid from Ireland, and myself . . .

I remember the Bridge. Not a sinner or a ghost, not a car or a bus, nothing at all to be seen but the empty bridge. Daniel himself was there, of course, and his monumental angels . . .

I spoke to him. It must have been Irish or English I spoke – because I haven't Latin, French, Greek or the language of the seagulls.

Whatever tongue I spoke, he took no notice of me. There's nothing I find more annoying than being given the deaf ear. I knew well that a bronzed man wasn't capable of much talk ... But couldn't he pretend? There's more ways of killing a dog than by hanging ... He could have spoken to my heart – and my heart is always open to receive pleasant tidings in a discreet fashion ...

He could have said that he had got my message, that he was grateful, that I should be going home now to my wife and family, if such I had ... or the likes. He'd have said all that if he were anyway decent ...

Since God granted me patience, something I've never ever got any credit for, I said to myself I'd give him another chance ...

"May God and Mary bless you, Daniel O'Connell," said I in the sweetest Gaelic of the Gaels of Ireland, word for word as my grandfather would have said it, and God rest him too; and they say the Irish spoken in his days is far superior to what it is now ... But if I spoke to him in the language of Brian Boru himself, the great Liberator was impervious to me.

"Well may God never put luck in your way," says I, angrily. I was going to give him a piece of my mind that would knock him off his pedestal. I was totally pissed off with him. I suppose anyone looking at me would say I was a proper madcap or, in civil service terms, out of order.

It wasn't long before I was surrounded by an unruly mob – they were coming at me from all sides. O'Connell's elite guard. I drew my silver-hilted sword before you could say "Emancipation".

"Lay down your sword in the name of the law," said one of them.

"Let ye stay the blade's length away from me," says I with a boldness to match.

"You've broken the law," says the other, "and we'll have to be taking you in."

"Ye won't be taking me in if ye're not taking yer man in," pointing to O'Connell, "or it's certain ye won't be having me without a fierce battle."

"We'll take him in too, only throw away your sword."

"All right so, if you swear before all present."

He swore. I threw away my sword. They leapt on me. They caught hold of me here and there. One fella grabbed my ear. I was thrown into the big, black car that people call the Black Maria. I was captured. Off she goes, Maria . . .

O'Connell was left behind in his victorious, stately posture. I wasn't too pleased with this injustice, for all their promises.

"Yeres is a crooked law," says I. They said nothing. "But it's not as crooked as yerselves . . ."

The answer to that was punches in the ribs and a barbecue sauce of rich expletives. I'd a sauce of my own to add to it. They made it clear that all the cursing and swearing was another case against me.

"If that's the way," says I, "I might as well earn it."

Every foul word, so to speak, that I ever heard since I left home became part of a litany – and I got a lovely "pray for us" in the ribs with each response. They didn't leave off until we arrived at the station – that's what they call it, the station. I call it the barracks. The drink had cooled down in me at this stage. I remember the barracks well. They dragged me into a back room. Three of them in front of me and one behind. The interrogation began. Name? Who are you? What have you in your pocket? . . . Are you a member of an illegal organization?

I was the master now, and would be until they got information from me – something I had no intention of giving them.

"Even if I had committed a crime, ye'd never find out by such a feeble line of questioning," I declared. One of them went bananas and gave it to me straight in the kisser. A half an hour they spent, beating me and questioning me. But I said nothing at all.

Eventually they lugged me down to a cell. I was given a blanket and ordered to go to sleep. With this I complied. I was just about to nod off on the hard wooden bed when I heard someone coming again. It was a middle-aged man this time. Far more civilized than the other lot. He was half-way towards being pleasant with me. But I wasn't going to be deceived – I remembered the way they tricked me before, not taking the Liberator in, as they had promised. But I knew, all the same, that they'd give me no rest.

"I'll say nothing tonight," I told him, "but if ye'll arrest O'Connell, as promised, maybe tomorrow after I've consulted my solicitor, maybe I'll talk then."

He was happy to get that much out of me. Off he went and that's all I can recall until the following morning. The court. That's what was facing me next day. I'd spent the morning being transferred from cell to cell. From car to car. The waiting was worse than the court itself . . .

I was first put into a cell in the courthouse. Two members of the travelling community there before me, asleep. Three wooden beds. I lay down on one. The great door opened. Tea, would you believe. The itinerants were quickly on their feet when they heard the tea coming. A small pot of tea and a slice of bread were placed near me. Up I stand like a crowing cock. I give the teapot a good old kick. The Guard says nothing at all. But I can see from the way he's looking at me that he won't forget – it will go on my account, as they might say in the bank . . .

I was called at last. I was brought to the bowels of the Courthouse. "Up you go now," says one of the Guards. Up I go. Into the court. The judge is there before me. A clerk by his side. Another clerk on the other side. Other state functionaries sitting by the wall, standing by the door. The audience seated behind me . . .

"So this is the nameless one," said the Judge.

"He is, your Honour," said the Guard, "he won't talk until he sees a solicitor and hmm . . . hmm . . ."

"Yes?"

"There's another condition as well, your Honour, but I'd rather not mention it at this time for fear it might raise laughter. I'll be asking for permission to have the case adjourned until . . . "

"And this other condition refers to –"

"The Special Crimes Act, your Honour."

"Case adjourned to the Special Court at high noon. Next!"

"Down. Down. Down," says the Guard.

Down again. Down the stairs. Up another stairs. Into another big cell already occupied by one detainee. They closed the door. Another wait. Exchange a few words with the other fella. I didn't bother with the lunch. The other man worried about the Special Court. Worst court in the world he said. The one with least mercy. The Judge with his name in Irish – if we appear before him it's a life sentence . . . A long wait. Listening to the other fella is punishment enough.

At long last the door opens. The other fella is taken out the door again. My turn to go down. I'm standing by the iron door of the court. In I go – the Guard with me every step of the way, like my shadow. What a shock. Sitting beside the Judge in all his composure, who should I see but the bould Daniel.

A little scarecrow of a man came up to me.

"I'll be speaking on your behalf," he said. "You say nothing except you're guilty. I'll do the talking. I know how these guys work. This is the Special Court. The Judge uses the Irish form of his name! You've only a squeak of a chance."

"How did they manage to bring yer man along?" I asked him, referring to the bould Dan.

"Special Branch. They can do that kind of thing . . ."

"Silence in the Court!"

"What's the charge?" asked the Judge with his name in Irish.

"Five in all, your Honour," said the Guard.

"Which are . . .?"

"One. Insulting a leading statesman in O'Connell Street Metropolitan. Two. Attacking a leading statesman in said street. Three. Attacking officers of the state in said street. Four. In possession of deadly weapon. Five. Resisting arrest."

"Guilty or not guilty?"

"Not guilty," said I.

"What did he say?"

"Guilty, your Honour," said the solicitor

"Has he ever been charged before?"

"Never, your Honour. My client comes from a very respectable background, incapable of imagining such offences. I request he be freed under The Probation Act . . ."

The Judge laughed.

"Let him go free so as to insult our statesmen, the Noble Gods of our ancestors, such as the heroic gentleman among us today, courtesy of the Special Branch? The Probation Act isn't worth sixpence in this Court. It is the act of Special Crimes we deal with here. Do you follow?"

"I follow, your Honour, but . . ."

"Life imprisonment," said the Judge and pounded the bench with such vehemence that O'Connell himself got a fright . . .

I was rehearsing a litany of abuse, seeing there was no more satisfaction to be got . . . But, I suppose, they were expecting as much. Suddenly I felt something like a towel gagging me . . . I was dragged down stairs. Then down another stairs. They knocked my skull in. That helped me to sleep.

translated by Gabriel Rosenstock

CELEBRATION

He was in the middle of the room. Lumps of people around him. Mmm . . . around him – but far away. Another mmm . . . He was far away? They were far away? What the hell. He was well used to being by himself at this stage. By now he could discern the haze of inhospitality that existed between them. Mmm . . .

He'd have to put up with it. Maybe he was in the middle of the room. What part of the world he couldn't say. This room was the whole world. A spacious room.

Tables. Chairs. Glasses. Posh delft. Posh voices. Posh friends. Legs. Hands. Mouths. Ear-rings. Cigarettes. Posh. Glasses.

Glasses especially. Being filled. Handed out. Breaths. Mingling one with the other. Sharing. Stomachs. Backsides. Swinging. Tight. Cute. Knees.

Twiddly bits. Fiddlesticks. Male gender. Female gender. Smoke rising. Up. In the middle of this big room. Says he, mmm . . .

Starry eyes. Shining. Small. Nice. Big. Nice. Friends, Romans, countrymen.

Concoction of desires. Glances of unmistakable allurement. Disguised by fiendishly clever winks of mild discretion. The shy suffocation of unknowable desire. Tender eyes.

Frolicsome fingers. Faces. Festivity.

And himself, says she, the distant one, mmm – with her bright eyes a-hunting she will go. Where is he. Or did he come at all, poor thing. Says she with the small, glowing eyes.

Oh, says she, the other one, with her small, knowledgeable eyes. He's here a long while. He's grand now. Lifting the veil of haze a fraction, theatrically, with nimble fingers, so the other could see. We're so proud of him. The wisps of haze fall reluctantly and fold and entwine in a passionate embrace! Entwined. Sparks of pure inhospitality being forged by the new time.

She rubbed her fairy fingers together. Her nose cocked. To the other: Now.

Oh, the eyes say once more. Isn't it blessed ye are. Who's himself.

I don't know. He doesn't be right. Not since the accident. He's not the only one. Says a voice. With uncertainty. God help him.

He's not the worst, says shining eyes. I'm not a hundred per cent myself. Whatever happened the poor divil. Says a voice. Some other voice. Nobody knows that. He could have fallen. He could. He could ... mmm ... have slipped.

The room is as stuffed as a turkey. Voices now. Hearty voices. Male. Female. Fondling each other. Joyously. Every voice. Every person. Gaiety. Volcanic spirits. Wreaths of smiles. Laughter in the blood. Heavenly intimations.

Maybe he was in the thick of them. A good-spirited placid individual, quite visible, approached him. You there. You'll have a drop of this. Aqua vitae.

I don't drink aqua vitae. I only drink aqua aeterna, come hell or high water. And I don't drink water.

But, says he, smiling, half-scuttered. I don't understand you. But I like you. For the occasion that's in it, old stock. Handing him a glass. He takes it. The glass in his fist.

Mmm ... tasting the drink. The pleasure-feeling compressing. More. The stuffing is coming out of the turkey. He could say nothing.

Shite and onions, says the unobnoxious one. Smiling pleasantly from his roseate face. Shite and onions. And goes.

There must be something big happening tonight or yesterday or the day before or the year before last. A celebration. There were lanterns lit. It must be tonight.

You'd never believe it. No one would believe.

He wouldn't believe it himself if his eyes didn't tell him. A miracle occurred. The haze of inhospitality was slowly disappearing. Little by little he was being un-bewitched. This night. Now people could accost him and talk to him, straight and crooked. From this side and that. And the other. Me, he said.

For the first time in ages voices were wrestling with his. Like everyone else, almost. He was capable of looking into eyes, effortlessly. They, too, could look into his. No bother. Taking him into their range of vision with open arms, almost. Did you ever see anything like it.

Is there any danger I'm in Heaven. Have a bit of sense, will you, he admonished himself. He laughed at the question and the answer.

He was content. Overjoyed even. The chair under his buttocks was satisfied. You'd know. The table as well. He was fit to dance. With sheer happiness. How lovely that everything in the room is so utterly content.

Giggly wiggly. His brain was getting active. Here, tonight, maybe he could make some sense of himself. Who he was. What it was that guided him into this palatial room stuffed with genial folk. They might tell him.

He was offered another drink. Some kind hand presented him with a glass. It was filled. He put the glass to his lips. It was delicious. A tonic.

No matter now. Last year doesn't count. You know well better than I do. But you can't say it because you haven't got the gift of poetry. Stop it. I'll have to continue.

Anything in the wide earthly world you want to say to me you can say to me now. I'm perfectly happy to listen. I love yez. My dear friends. Ye goddesses. Ye good people. All of yez.

I suppose, she said, with her voice . . . O, I dunno who she is, I never saw her before tonight . . . O, indeed I did, many's the time, she said in that strange whisper of her eyes – your're glad to be here. If it weren't for me, she said with unwavering certainty, there'd be none of this generosity, I'm telling you. I'm good for you.

Well now, I don't recall who you are. Never mind, says she. Good luck. May you live to be a hundred.

A hundred? I'm not in Heaven so. He laughs.

Was she laughing? He didn't know. I'll be back in a tick, she says. I'd like to exalt you. We'll try to exalt you.

Don't get it. She's gone.

Generosity. Says me, to himself what the feck is going on. The echo of the goddess's voice still hovers: to exalt you, exalt you. He that humbleth himself shall be exalted, at any rate. It doesn't matter. Merrily.

Merrily. Shall I live now.

Then. A melodious voice. Pure music. Ambrosia. Dripping from every syllable. Honey. Temptation. Fullness. Heat. He'd heard it before.

In some previous harmonious existence. The voice said nothing. Nothing to say. The voice was all.

The wheel goes round.

Men responding to women. The natural law. Natural legitimate attraction.

Let's get out of here, are you coming. This voice, from this face, more loving still.

Why so, says he.

Oh, says she, her hand touches him, replying in a legitimate natural smile.

I don't get it. Stammer.

You don't have to get it, says she. Just taste. She takes his hand, says she.

I miss her touch.

But, says I. Nothing. But I didn't say it. Another but. Why is every woman so soft, so loving! So melodious, desirous, generous with me tonight.

Because we like you a lot, tonight.

Can't be. I don't remember anything like this before. I remember nothing. I know nothing. Says I, says he.

We like you – because women like men, I think. Law of nature, I think.

Old men, too.

Sure, old men.

That's not right. That can't be right.

Keep it under your hat so, says she. She wasn't laughing.

And her face disappeared among a sea of bright faces.

Then, pain. The stab of emptiness.

The crowd began to lose all contour. He took a drink. He knew he'd be better for it. And another delicious sip. Soon he'll be in heaven again. We'll call it heaven. Says he. He was laughing.

Generosity, he said. Maybe like a present on one's birthday. It must be somebody's birthday.

Present. Christmas present. That's what it's all about. It's Christmas. Do you think?

Is it Christmas?

Christmas, said a big, plump, rosy-cheeked bespectacled gentleman. Christmas. Ha, ha, ha! Merry Christmas everybody. Ho, ho, ho! You never lost it, he said. Placing his hand on his shoulder. Why would you, he said. You're a great man.

You're as good, says he, as any man I've ever seen. Good man yourself.

The big burly man lifted a bottle and poured another drop into the glass.

Knock that back, old son. You well deserve it . . . you deserve a woman, said the big fellow staring lustfully across at two lovely knees, bare and elegantly parted, making themselves known. Ha ha. It's many a good deed I've done. My list of accomplishments is endless.

If I'd the time I'd tell you how good I was. There's nothing I like better, said he in the silent, secretive tongue of the mind, than performing feats. What a pity I haven't the time. But talk isn't what's on my mind at the moment . . . ha, ha, says he, making his way over towards the super-attractive knees.

He left me there, he said.

But he wasn't alone quite yet. Another face lit up in his presence. More honest, he thought, than the rest. Not as virtuous. That's the way he read her physiognomy. But she was friendly with him. Against her will, he thought. Maybe the happy atmosphere here tonight caused her to be friendly.

But, she says.

Yes.

A little laugh. I've something to tell you. You shouldn't be here.

Why is that?

It was wrong of you to come.

I didn't come.

Oh, and to be sure you did. The big man got the better of you. He hoodwinked you. It's a game he plays. He'll be able to say you came to him. That you were happy. That you participated in his festivities. Alas.

I don't get it.

It's not easy. You'll never find out now. I know the law. Long days of misfortune stretch before you. He has you by the short and curlies.

The big burly friendly fellow.

He can be friendly. But that's no use to you. You'll have to wait. You shouldn't have come.

I couldn't help it. I didn't know a thing. I don't know who I am myself.

You've been cheated, I think, she said, with a sympathetic smile. But maybe the fault was partly your own.

I was very happy tonight until you arrived.

Be happy, she said, angrily. I'm off.

Don't go. I prefer you.

But I'm not a member. I wouldn't be allowed on much longer. You should never have come at all. But you'll be happy enough.

She lifted the bottle and poured a drink in his glass.

That's a powerful drink, isn't it, she said, smiling nervously. She was uncertain about something.

There's no love in this place, she said, I have to go. There's no place for me here. Not that I would want that there should be.

He lowered his head. He didn't want to be watching her leaving him.

translated by Gabriel Rosenstock

SOMEONE ELSE

How oft, oft, often I've traipsed up and down that street. How often? And still I didn't know all that was going on. That's a great thing about a street; you'll never know the half of it.

In the end I came to live there, having spent the best part of my life going through it and who knows how many shoes it has worn out. I thought I knew it like the back of my hand and could sail through it with my two eyes closed. But whatever I thought, the street was a street. It was as streetly as you'd find anywhere, streetlier if the truth be told. I was to find that out, later.

Memories returned of days long gone. I thought of a friend who lived on that street. I remembered his name. I remembered the house. Though I was never inside, I recalled the door. The posh varnish on it. A fashionable design at the time, imitation Chinese calligraphy. My friend was terribly proud of it.

The door is no more. Nor my friend, nor his people. Nor the records he lent me and that I had little interest in. Nor the records I gave him and that he had little interest in.

Isn't that youth for you. And doesn't it be in an awful hurry to go. Zip!

When I came to live on the street, the sister-in-law began to get interested in this area of the city. Whatever it was came over her. I suppose it had something to do with the stories I had of the place. You know the way one sheep follows another.

She thought the street had some magic or other. She couldn't praise it highly enough. She wanted to settle down there. It appears she believes in destiny because she announced that the street was linked to her karma. Nothing would deter her, man or God.

And it happened, as though arranged by heavenly influence, that a house on the street came on the market. The paint on the *for sale* sign was hardly dry and the sister-in-law haggling. And then she discovered a few things that weren't to her liking.

The crowd that were selling the house were leaving because of the next-door neighbour. Not that there was anything untoward, you understand, it's just that they weren't too happy. It was hard to pin down. They were selling at a ridiculously low price and no more was to be said. The sister-in-law didn't know if she was delighted or horrified. She was between two minds and vacillated thus for a spell.

She had big plans, of course. The type of plans that get into people's heads every seven years. Total renewal! It was more than a dose of the fidgets, you understand. But the plans had to be momentarily stalled in the light of this new intelligence. She was to be pitied, yes.

She's a broad-minded one. You have to say that about her. There's nothing sanctimonious about her. Nor is she uppity.

She'll tell you so herself. Sure, she says, it's too much like hard work keeping your nose in the air all the time. She doesn't believe in unnecessary drudgery.

One night there was a few of us sitting in the corner of the bar. Chin-wagging, rehydrating ourselves and letting the world drift idly by, you understand. And we started – or one of us – talking about houses; we were half-gone, but we were still all there. An artist, I think it was, who set the ball rolling. He hadn't been a resident all that long but what he didn't know you could write on the back of a stamp. You know the kind of chap. What he didn't know wasn't worth talking about.

Life is pretence, nothing else, that's what he said. Look at the house below that's for sale. Nobody's buying it because the house next door is a shambles and the tatterdemalion that's in it. You'd think the poor old man was some kind of an ogre or something the way they're talking. Sure he's as perfectly harmless as a lamb in April.

Not only that – another expert put in his say – sure he hasn't long to go, the poor craythur, hasn't he an ailing heart. And we all know the way he looks after himself!

These nuggets of information and theorizing were most interesting. As far as my sister-in-law was concerned, that put a new complexion on matters.

She decided to buy the house. We understood the reasoning behind her decision, though not putting it into so many words.

She'd get the house for a song. After a while, maybe not that long, when God would decide to provide a more spacious mansion in his glorious kingdom for the wretch next door, new owners would move in and put some shape on the shell he left behind. This, of course, would enhance her own house and attract customers to the café she intended to open. Even if God didn't extend his invitation next week, it would be fine. It would give her the opportunity to start converting the house to her purposes.

She was overjoyed. Now at last her ambitious plans could be realized. She thanked God.

Days followed nights. Birds went nest-building, or renovating. They had plans of their own. Rivers ran.

She fixed up the house. After her own fashion. Putting her stamp on it. The house was her alpha and omega. The core of the universe. Her place.

She smiled incessantly. All her plans were fitting into shape. All the right steps in the right direction.

She thought it was time to give it the appearance of a café. She acquired all the necessary thingamabobs. She asked for help and advice. She got it. It was plain sailing.

At last, everything was ready for the opening. She was advised to bide her time for a while, until after Christmas maybe. Do you think? she said.

Well now, all her advisers and ready hands declared, we don't want to discourage you or anything, but the house next door is as ramshackled as ever and the broken door gaping out at your own and the raggedy fellow talking to himself and giving out to himself most of the time. It wouldn't be right or proper having a café next to that. Leave it be a while, girl.

Fair enough. She'd stick it out another while. What harm. Time enough. Anyway, wasn't Christmas coming. Busy days ahead. Yes siree and nights of festive revelry. Ah well, that's the way it is.

Rivers ran and ran.

Christmas was over and the new year getting on its feet and the world was progressing. Some, however, could not continue any more.

We had heard that the old man had taken a weakness. He was out in the cold in the other end of town on some errand or other and he caught a bad chill. Real bad.

Next thing we know, the funeral arrangements are being made. Poor man.

The sister-in-law was quite shook, really. She's a sensitive soul behind it all. A Christian.

She said nothing. Nothing was said. The days went by, days of wine, days of vinegar.

The street's the same as ever. Noisy. Bustling. Hithering and thithering. What does that street care who's alive or dead, who walks, who paces, who rushes, who crawls, come rain, hail or sunshine?

My sister-in-law was thinking of her own affairs. It's an ill wind, as they say, and it had blown.

She began preparing for the day. The café would soon be open. Her dream was coming true and she'd be awake for it!

I don't know what my circle of acquaintances is up to, what they do with their lives. Even if they told me, I'd probably forget. But I do notice the odd thing, microscopically.

I was somewhat astounded that the café hadn't opened. Nothing was said. The house next door didn't have the *for sale* sign up, as predicted.

It wasn't my business but I made it my business and went in search of the sister-in-law. I'd ferret out the low-down on the situation.

If there was anything to know. There was. She didn't know what was happening next door. People were coming and going for a month and the house hadn't gone on the market yet. You have to be patient. These things always take time.

She said she was content to wait. So it goes.

I took giant strides up the street, something I often do. What should I see but the *for sale* sign. But I had to look twice. I had to clean my glasses. I had to cross the street, with all the traffic and all, to see if my eyes were deceiving me.

I was right first time round. I saw something that wouldn't please the sister-in-law. The *for sale* sign had been erected over her own door. The auctioneers had blundered, seemingly. The twits. Wait till she sees it. She'll tongue-lash them to kingdom-come. I'll say that much about her. She's particular and any kind of codology rouses her something terrible.

I knocked on the door to give her the news, if she was in. She wasn't. I headed off. Yerra, I went into the bar.

In the door and who should I see but the artist. Oddly enough, I got the distinct impression that he was trying to avoid me, like maybe he owed me money or something like that. I went up to him because it didn't matter to me at that moment whether he owed me a few bob or not. I cornered him.

I put the question to him, eye to eye, he being the authoritative source of all local news. What's this about the *for sale* sign or what's going on at all? Oh! The sign above the door?

He told me to sit down and take it easy. It had nothing to do with him. Who said it had? I'm not blaming you for anything, my good man.

This *for sale* sign was correctly positioned, he informed me. It's not so! It is. She's selling. She'd getting rid of the house as soon as ever possible. Moving out.

Why this sudden change of heart? Well, there's a reason, a good reason. That's what he said, and he knows what's going on down around here.

I had to polish my spectacles again. I felt like having an ear-wash as well, to make sure I was hearing what I heard.

Do you know what happened, says he. When the old fella croaked it they found out – and very few knew about this – that there was someone else in the house. Someone who never went out. A younger brother, a proper lout. The old man was his slave. You know they way it is. He has no intention of selling the house or giving it a lick. You understand.

I did.

I was thinking of the sister-in-law. I wouldn't be seeing her in these parts again very often.

She wouldn't be too keen to see any of us, he said. I wouldn't like to meet her now, he said.

To tell you the truth, neither would I; not for a good while yet.

translated by Gabriel Rosenstock

ALAN TITLEY

Corkonian, educated in Coláiste Chríost Rí in Cork city. Later trained as a primary-school teacher in Coláiste Phádraig, Drumcondra, Dublin, where he now runs the Irish Department. Taught for some time in Africa and in a school for deaf boys in Dublin. He is best known as a novelist, but is also an acclaimed short-story writer, playwright and critic.

THE JUDGEMENT

Adam heard the music first. I thought it was a ghetto-blaster or some music store trying to flog their latest wares.

"Listen!" said Adam. "I think he's out of tune."

"Bloody sure he's not bloody Eddie Calvert," said I, plucking a name out of the past. "He wouldn't get a job with a bloody bad brass band."

I had to admit I didn't feel that well since early morning. A shiver down my backbone and a quiver up my thigh-bone told me it wasn't going to be a lucky or a sunshiny day. The alarm clock failed to go off, Docila slept through, the children were late for school and a molar started acting up. The last time I felt as lousy as this the boss called me in and gave me a rise. This only went to prove I couldn't believe either my hunches or my bones.

Adam and myself were hoping to have a quiet lunch in the restaurant on the corner of the street but when he heard the music he gave me a dig in the ribs. There were others who noticed it also. Some grinned, some grimaced, all turned around looking for the music. I saw two guys starting to dance on the street but the rhythm screwed them up and they shagged off. I saw an old fellow scrunching the butt of a fag and hiding it under his coat despite the heat of the day.

Even though we were both starving we had to stop and listen. We thought the music was coming from the next street but when we went looking for it we always discovered it was still just one street away.

"Listen to that," said a stranger next to me. "You'd think we had enough electioneering by now. Lies and promises, promises and lies! What more are they good for?"

"Election, my arse," said someone else, "stay where you are and you'll see the greatest show on earth. Didn't you hear that the circus is coming to town?"

"It's all one big circus anyway," said Adam, not entirely seriously. He was like that when he wanted to. We gave as good as we got when we needed to, but for some reason I felt a big grey lump growing quietly in my gut.

White fluffs of cloud dabbed the sky but they didn't cross the sun. I looked up to see two helicopters like fireflies racing above the city. I imagined by their frenzy that a bank had been robbed or terrorists had escaped from some prison and were now on the run. And then they vanished as if they had never fluttered above the roofs of the houses.

"Come on," said Adam, grabbing me by the elbow. "Let's split. We can't spend the day staring at the sky. Fuck 'em all. Let's stuff our guts and let them all piss off."

I was a bit reluctant to leave as long as there was a hullabaloo in the streets but hunger and convention won out. We sat down at the table where we had our lunch for nearly twenty years. We had a good view of the streets in case it was a *coup d'état* or the boys were back in town.

"Just imagine the tanks rolling by," said Adam, his mouth watering while he enjoyed and took pleasure from the thought . "I'd give anything just for ten minutes of absolute power. Just ten minutes."

"What would you do?" I asked, wondering about his grasp of the conditional mood.

"I have a little list," he said, speaking in a conspiratorial hush in case anyone with big ears was listening. "I have been compiling it for years. Every politician, every journalist, every sports commentator who has been a pain in the ass, they're all on the list."

"It must be quite long so," I said.

"As long as a wet day in County Mayo," he said. "I'd put them all into one big enormous tub. A huge transparent vat with a hole at the top just big enough for one person to go through simultaneously and at the same time."

"You have been thinking about this for a while," I said, as if I didn't know. It was always interesting to see if he had another turn of the screw or if anybody had been added to the list.

"Do you see that crane?" he asked, pointing his spoon in the direction of the tall construct waving about above the City Hall like a scorpion's tail about to strike. "I'd hang my specially designed state-of-the-art tub off the top of that and do the hippy-hippy shakes up and around and topsy-turvy and head over heels so that just one of my chosen list would fall out, one at the time. That is the circus that I want. Just ten minutes."

"Well, bully for you," I said, thinking of my own list, "but I'm afraid that whenever the *coup* comes neither you nor I will have much to do with it."

"Speak for yourself," he said, calling the waiter for something or other. "I have military training just as well as you. You can't put that one over on me."

"Five weeks in the FCA twenty years ago! I know of some petty dictators who still wouldn't have us. When the tanks roll up I'm going to stay sitting here smoking my cigar."

If this was bullshit we were under the illusion it was good bullshit, and anyway if we couldn't pass muster we could at least pass the time. We all got whanged by life's vicissitudes but we still had our middle-aged dreams to keep us warm. Our ship would come in, or we would find the crock of gold at the end of the garden, or we would fall in love with a rich Jewish princess. Or at any rate we could keep talking as long as we had no other choice and there was no other thing to do nor any other place to go. O yes, we had our complaints, but it was better to curse the darkness than light a penny candle on a star.

"You better stuff yourself with that apple tart," I said to Adam, having nothing better to say, "you won't get anything as good as it until tomorrow. There's nothing worse than pangs of hunger in the smack-bang-middle of the high afternoon."

He would do that anyway without any encouragement from me, but that didn't mean we were in any great hurry to pack up and go. To be on duty was not the same thing as to be in work. We still had time to gabble about the Ex-President's mistress, the humour of the financial pages, ecological holidays in Greenland, the etymological derivation of the exclamation mark, the man who died of a broken fart which was great gas, and the pimp who thought everything was great crack. We paid a fortune for our lunch in order to help the economy as we did every day and we wearily wended our way back to the office.

Out on the street everyone was on the move. They all looked as if they were going in the same direction. There was a look in their eyes which had never been there before. You knew that even if you had never seen them until now. I tried to talk to one young fellow but he stared at me from out of eyes that welled up in tears.

Adam tried to chat up one woman but she laughed at him with a nervous highly-strung laugh.

I grabbed one old wrinkly by the elbow but he shook me off with a viciousness which I scarcely thought he could have.

Adam spoke to a child but no wisdom came forth from his mouth.

"Has the government fallen?" I shouted to the crowd.

"Fallen, my arse," said one guy with a wart on his nose and vanished in the great wash.

"Has the stock market collapsed?" Adam pleaded, because he could be quite sensitive about these moneyed things when he had to be.

"Fuck the stock," said another guy who looked to be about a thousand years old and never enjoyed a day in his life.

"Have the Brits attacked?" I shouted, falling back on the old enemy in time of necessity, but I only got an emphatic "Not at this time" from a woman who was sucking her thumb.

"He's over there!" screamed a man between horrors and hosannas who had a rosary beads or a knuckle-duster wrapped around his fist, and pointed us with his whole body to the corner of the road where we thought we had first heard the music.

"Who is it?" we both asked in unison and together, scarlet butterflies rising in our stomachs.

"This is the day I have been waiting for since the beginning of time," the man said, and then grabbed us by the dirty scruff of our necks and shoved us forward to where the crowd was gawping up at the building.

"This is it now," said your man, as happy as a kid going in to see Santa Claus, "you're all fucked, you shower of fucking fuckers. Thanks be to God!"

"Who is he?" I asked, even plaintively, about the guy standing on the corner of the upper window who looked as if he was about to jump. "Why doesn't somebody get the ambulance or the Gardaí? If he falls he'll make an awful mess."

"Shut your face, you fool," said your man again, a smile like a flea's arse flitting across his face. "There's no chance of him falling. Don't you see his wings?"

He was, unfortunately, right. I had been paying attention to the trumpet in his right hand and to his unusual get-up and I hadn't noticed the two golden wings sticking out behind his back.

"Jaysus, I know who it is," said Adam, nearly licking my ear, "it's fucking Goldie Horn."

I suppressed a chuckle as nobody else was chuckling, and anyway, this was real serious public shit rather than simple private angst.

"Or maybe it's Icarus," I retorted. "He's probably forgotten that we have aeroplanes for the last hundred years."

"Judas Icarius," said Adam, "give him enough rope to hang himself."

"It is written also," said your man "that thou shalt not go free because this is the day of accounting."

"We had those accountants in last week," said Adam, "and they were some accuntants."

Just then Willie Wings on the window let a great blast from his trumpet and everybody jumped back in horror. He laid down his trumpet and did produce a big red book from within his breast and commenced to read.

"Districts seven and eight," he proclaimed, in a voice that had a certain eastern accent to it, "that is to say, Cabra, Phibsboro, Arbour Hill, Stoneybatter, Inchicore, The Coom, The South Circular Road and adjacent areas, Section A; Districts three and nine, Clontarf, Ballybough, Clonliffe, Drumcondra, Whitehall, Santry and Griffith Avenue, Section B; Districts five and thirteen, Coolock, Artane, Raheny, Bayside, Barrytown, Sutton, Donamede and Baldoyle, Section C; Districts one and six, Ranelagh, Rathmines, Rathgar, Terenure and Harold's Cross, Section D; District four, Donnybrook, Ballsbridge, Sandymount, Sandycove and Ringsend, Section E; Districts ten and eleven, Ballyfermot and Blanchardstown, Section F; District eighteen, Cabinteely, Foxrock, Cornelscourt . . ."

People began moving away as their districts were called out, some obviously despondent, others proud and haughty, but nobody was saying very much. Whatever sounds there were came from the buzz of the announcements and the shuffle of feet beginning to move into the distance.

"Where are you?"

"Section E I think. I hear we'll get our entry cards at the gates."

"What about the wife and kids?"

"It's everyone for himself now. That's the rule. Anyway they will have heard by now."

"I don't know if I'm suitably dressed. My mother always told me to have clean underwear on me in case of an accident, or unforeseen circumstances. Maybe this is what she was warning me about."

I turned around when I heard the newsboy shouting about the evening papers. The first edition was out earlier than usual because of the news.

"*Herald* or *Press*," he roared, his voice reaching new heights of excitement. "End of the world news! End of the world this afternoon! Official statement from Heaven! Last judgement in the Phoenix Park!"

I shoved him the price of the paper and Adam looked in over my shoulder. According to their religious correspondent angels were landing in different locations all over the country since midday proclaiming the news. Judgement had already been given in most other European countries. The heavenly host was moving with the sun and wouldn't reach America until early in the morning Irish time. I suppose there was no such thing any more as Irish time but it was difficult to get rid of the old metaphors. There was no hard data as yet available from the rest of the European Union because all the fax lines were clogged up and the Internet was acting funny. There was a small diagram at the bottom of the second page which purported to show unconfirmed figures for the number of saved and the number of damned in each country so far. It gave us some satisfaction to see that good Catholic countries like Spain and Portugal and even Italy had the highest saved rate. But Adam said that they also were the biggest producers of red wine, and that was the real reason. Against that there was a very high damnation rate in awful Protestant countries like Germany, Denmark and Finland, but England was the worst of all.

"Eighty-four per cent!" said Adam, in wonder and not a little satisfaction. "That won't leave much room for us, thanks be to Jaysus."

"Any mention of Purgatory?" I mentioned, scanning the page up and down, "or the likes of Limbo?"

There wasn't, but there was more than enough speculation about who amongst the great and mighty and the eminent greasies of the country would go up and who would go down. The journalists were very kind to themselves but more than nasty to politicians whom they didn't like. They weren't too sure about the Cardinal as he had criticized the press the week before, but they did admit that if the Pope was saved that he had a very good chance also. I supposed this was an attempt to be fair now that the end was nigh. There was a full page of the detailed arrangements – the various routes to the Park, parking lots, the sites of the different pens into which people were to go, the tents of the Red Cross, fish and chip stalls, beer tables, bookies stands, photographers, toilets.

"They all seem to be walking anyway," I said, as we had failed to hail a taxi, "let's go."

We hit the road and joined the throng making its way to the Phoenix Park. Most of the people were quiet and reflective although there was the occasional murmur of prayer and the jangle of a rosary beads. Dublin Bus was providing a special cheap knock-down one-way fare but most people seemed to want to walk. I suppose it gave them a chance to stop and think every so often and to examine the state of their souls. Others were going back over the course of their lives trying to put it all together. The humour improved as we went on, however. We heard an occasional nervous laugh as if people were practising confessions on one another.

"Do you remember?" Adam asked me reflectively, "do you remember you asked me once what would I do if I knew the end of the world was coming? Remember that?"

"I was talking about the Third World War then," I said. We were passing by Phibsboro at this time and the road was getting congested at the major junction. "We all thought it would happen that way. But I suppose since the Russians and Americans decided against frying us all God decided he'd have his pound of flesh anyway."

"It's just as the poet said: 'This is the way the world will end, this is the way the world will end, this is the way the world will end, not with a bang but with a wimpey.'"

"And you said you'd go mad around the streets rubbing and robbing and plundering and whoring and fucking and blinding and doing all those things that only crawl under the skin of civilization. And I said I'd blow my head off with a gun. Funny that we don't want to do any of those things now."

"Life must go on," he said wearily, "that's the way it is – so it goes."

"Last few ices, last few ices," a vendor shouted, "anyone now for the last few ice-creams." He pushed his way through the crowd with skilled and sharp elbows.

There was a small bunch of angels standing guard outside Glasnevin Cemetery as we were going by. They had their golden swords drawn and had their backs to us. We thought this was a bit unusual until we saw them holding back the crowd inside. A motley collection of emaciated corpses, rotting bodies, skeletons, stiffs, cadavers and carcasses jostled at the gates trying to get out. It must have been that they were looking for a second chance. I have to say that they were not suitably attired to join the likes of us on our way to the general judgement.

"Do you see de Valera?" shouted one woman, pointing out a lanky tall skeleton peering longingly through the bars of the gates.

"He hasn't changed much, anyway" said another.

"Except that he's a bit straighter now than he ever was," said a third.

"So much for the treaty," somebody mumbled.

"Who called him a traitor?"

There might have been a row only somebody joked that he could hardly be called the devil incarnate now, which drew the reply that he was at least the devil of Éire.

There were others who swore that they saw Roger Casement who would certainly know his way to the Phoenix Park; and yet others who said that it had to be Daniel O'Connell arguing with the angels with big rhetorical flourishes in the hope that he might be let out. Maybe he thought he had one more big speech in him before a captive audience.

We didn't have time to follow the discussion as we were swept along in the tide of people away from the tide of history. It might have been interesting to have them along. They could have told us all that stuff the biographers never dug up. Ah well.

"Isn't it enough for any one of us to be living in the present for none of us can be living forever and we must be satisfied," said Adam, taking the words out of my mind. But he said many other things also which are not the matter of this story but which might be worth telling by somebody else some other time.

When we reached the gates of the Phoenix Park the crowds were as thick as flies on a summer eve. They were coming from every direction, some on their own, some with their families, some with their second families, some others uncertainly with their present partners of similar gender or bent. Life was still ours but the future which beckoned was short. Guardian angels were posted every few yards giving directions and orders as required. We were all given identification cards on the other side of the Zoological Gardens. It would certainly be tragic if anyone was sent to hell as a result of mistaken identity.

The great blue sky was awash with music as we approached the centre of the park. Those cherubim and seraphim must have been practising for aeons and aeons just for this one day. I couldn't quite see them yet but I could hear the brass and the boom and the hosannas and hallelujahs. I was lucky to be still with Adam although I must admit that Docila and the children did fleetingly cross my mind. If I didn't see them this side of the judgement it was unlikely I would see them on the other.

We had red cards and we followed all the directions until we got to our pen. We were made sit on long wooden benches and told to wait until we were called. The odd vendor had sneaked in and was attempting to sell Coke or orange-juice because it was a hot day. The angels didn't seem to bother too much about them. I think they were more worried about the ones who were trying to duck back in the queue and were giving bribes to people with holier faces. They were also trying to ensure that we kept our eyes glued on the giant movie screens that were posted around us showing different pictures. I was hoping to get a glimpse of the Judge and the throne and what was happening in the centre of the action but that didn't seem to be coming up yet. To tell you the truth they were quite interesting. We had a choice of about seven different screens but we could only concentrate on one at a time.

The one I was looking at was a kind of horror movie. For a moment

I thought it was a video of what was going on in another part of the park. There were angels in it, I remember. Seven of them if I recall correctly. They had trumpets and were preparing to blow them. When the sound of the first trumpet was heard I did see a beast coming up out of the sea, having seven heads and ten horns, and upon its head ten diadems and curses spewing out of the mouths of the seven heads. And then another one blew his trumpet and I saw as it were a sea of glass mingled with fire and the fire was licking the rims of the mountains and the people were climbing up the mountains to escape from the fire. And when the third angel blew his trumpet the mountain rose up and crashed down into the sea and the sea became blood and swallowed up all the boats and the fish. This was like unto *Krakatoa east of Java*, only better! Then a star fell from Heaven to earth and opened up a bottomless pit, and the pit belched up smoke that threw up poisonous scorpions and hydra-headed monsters and cookie zombies with papier mâché make-up that wouldn't convince anyone. Grand if you like that kind of stuff but I felt it had all been done before. The producer of this movie wasn't very subtle, and anyway I don't think it scared anybody.

I suppose the idea was that it would pass the time and divert our attention from the moving queues going past us to the place of judgement. We tried to stand up every so often in order to stretch our limbs but we were really trying to get a glimpse of the bench.

"Did you see him yet?" Adam asked me, after I did a little hop and a jump.

"I don't think so," I said, "he appears to be entirely surrounded by the Deitorium Guards. I think he's tall, slender, blonde, bearded and blue-eyed."

"He has no beard," a wise-looking guy next to me said, speaking as if he really knew something that the rest of us didn't. "He's as bald as a baby's bum, as well-dressed and groomed as any chief executive of a big company."

"I heard that," said a red-headed man courteously, "and I beg to oppose. I saw him a few moments ago and he was big, fat and hairy. Quite like the Pope actually, apart from his fine head of hair."

"Ye're all wrong ye ignorant slobs!" A woman was standing on a seat wringing her hands and mouthing at us in a brassy voice. "She's a woman I'm telling ye! A big strong power-dressed woman with glasses! I saw her."

"Yes, and I suppose she is black too, and wears a 'Save the Whales' button, and is eating a macrobiotic sandwich," I said, but I don't think anyone heard me. They were too busy holding forth about what God looked like but I think in the end we had to agree that nobody had really seen him. A few people might have got clocked if it wasn't for the angelic police keeping a close eye on us. Adam said he was a bit pissed off with all this theology stuff although he did admit he was getting excited at the prospect of meeting Him. If it was only that He was the biggest cheese of all in the history of the world and that he wanted to satisfy his own curiosity.

When we saw the people in the pen next to us getting up and being organized into queues we knew our time was not long off. They were moving along so briskly that it dawned on me there could have been more than one judge, or else he had a few assistants like Santa Claus at Christmas. Or else again that you didn't get much chance to plead your case. Maybe it was all written down in the Big Book of Judgement and your fate was sealed ever before you got to the bench.

A strange quietness came upon us and the banter died away as we were told to stand up and be ready. This was the day and the hour of which we didn't know. I gritted my teeth and a weird tingle went down my spine when we were ordered into our queue for the long walk along the beaten track of the green, green grass to where our home would be decided. Now was the time for examining our conscience for the last time and weighing up the good with the bad. I remembered all my vices with some affection – pride, covetousness, lust, gluttony, anger, envy and sloth – but I couldn't say I was particularly good at any one of them. I also had many virtues, but it would be a vice to enumerate them. If there was sometimes evil in my heart there was also charity. I had no machine with which to weigh them against one another, however. How could you measure cigarettes and whiskey and wild, wild women against doing your duty and saying your prayers and voting for the government? Anyway, I'd soon know the answer. The same questions must have been bugging Adam because he had got very quiet. Or maybe he had just remembered some big bad sin that had escaped him until now.

The queue stretched out as far as my eyes could see, yea, nearly unto the ends of the park. There seemed to be still millions packed into the pens on each side of us, and needless to say they weren't green with envy. We got prodded with batons every so often to keep us moving, and I even saw one guy getting thumped by an angel for dawdling. After a while the judgement area began to become clearer but we were still too far away to guess what was happening. I was amazed how quickly we were moving, almost like a Sunday afternoon stroll.

"Make way! Make way!" a guard shouted at us and pushed us to one side rather roughly. A huge lorry was making its way along the track and was being driven by two angels. Its siren went through our ears like glass cutting through bone. It swept past us in a swirl of dust and we were allowed crawl back into the centre of the passageway.

"What was that all about?" I heard one guy ask impatiently.

"Did you not see what was on the back of the lorry?"

"Skins," said somebody or other, "I saw another few lorries just like that when I was coming in a few hours ago. One of the angels told me they were sheep- and goatskins. We are all given one or the other of them after sentence has been passed – depending on where we are going."

"It was mostly goatskins so on that last load." This much was spoken by a large lugubrious mountain of a man for whom any kind of a fitting would have been a professional challenge for the heavenly tailors. "They must be in great demand." This much spoken resignedly.

I should have been surprised by the petty conversation going on all around me but I wasn't. Life was too important to be left to the philosophers. I overheard one woman asking her friend if she thought God would be as good-looking or as sexy as Brad Pitt, but then she suddenly remembered she had forgotten to hang out the wash. What looked to me like a fancy rugger-bugger was discussing his golf handicap with another guy who was only interested in car upholstery. A priest ahead of us spent his time looking into a pocket mirror and combing his hair. There were, of course, others whose faces were ashen and drawn as if they knew that the wages of sin were about to be paid. On the other hand there wasn't much point in throwing yourself on the ground with wailing and gnashing of teeth.

"Would you mind if I went first, I mean go ahead of you?" Adam asked me as we began to approach the judgement throne.

"Would I mind?" I said incredulously. "Of course you can. Those few seconds might make all the difference between everlasting torment and an eternity of celestial bliss. Go ahead!"

By this time we could get a good look at the judgement throne and at God himself. There was a huge angel standing on his right-hand side. He was wearing formal evening clothes with a green carnation in the lapel. A big leather-bound volume was open before him. There were a few other angels lolling about the throne also but they were obviously getting bored with everything. Two lines stretched out on both sides behind the throne but it was clear that the one to the left with the people wearing the goatskins was much longer than the other. The angel giving out the sheepskins was more or less redundant.

Our ears were pricked up the closer we got to the interrogation. It was difficult to follow every word at first but I soon began to get the gist of it. It appeared that God would say something, and then the angel would ask a question and the person would be whisked away after that. I found myself hiding behind Adam, but I knew that I couldn't get away with that for long.

"I see you're not wearing a tie," I heard the angel say to a teenager just a little bit ahead of us, "go to hell!"

"In the hoond of the cakes, purples or aflamed with cloaks," I heard God say to the next guy, "foreplicate that forum, O Muckle."

"God says that you're all right," the angel said stretching out a hand towards the heap of sheepskins, "I'm told you went to the right school."

"Oily zounds!" God said, looking at the nice young woman who was next, "bydeboils alanna buddy hast a vein twinpeekaboozies and whale clonking doanlast didgiridoo. Dattbee a through ghostspill, you bedda boleweevil me!"

"Bye-bye, farewell, *auf Wiedersehen*, good-night," said Muckle the angel to her, "he didn't like your clothes. Next!"

The next up was an elderly man who looked scholarly and pious. He took off his hat and curtsied politely.

"Who the fofo costuree me?" said God, "a burden in the bosh wotnot joice addlerup pound for pound. Amon aye right? 'Botchito ergo sum' samizdat I pray tallways."

"Put on your goatskin," said Muckle, "you ain't got no ticket for Heaven. You should have bought it when you had the chance. It's too late now."

"Whoroo the lustie dabbie plunking the plushty?" God asked the next young girl, who had obviously put on her very best dress for the occasion. "Or oroo the chickybiddy whang woofs the woost waddie joke buzzer? Whorov the squidge and squish ovdat hah!"

"He has just asked you if you know the third law of thermodynamics," said Muckle interpreting for her, "but as it is perfectly plain that you haven't the least clue you better fuck off down to hell."

I was looking very carefully at the priest because if anyone had a passport he surely did. He stood up directly and made a brief humble bow before turning his head ever so slightly towards the judgement throne. God looked kindly down on him and smiled widely from ear to ear showing a perfectly formed row of golden teeth.

"I om the Ram of Gob," he said, "and thee pissed a balls prophet. The dimple tooth you buggerup and you bekim alloy for alloy. As furry high cough earned ukan shakov. Jew dearme?"

"But I spread your word, I preached the gospel," the priest protested, as he didn't really need a translation, "I kept all the commandments, I followed the truth . . ."

"The truth?" Muckle snorted, turning towards God with a query on his brow, "what is this truth thing of which he speaks?"

"Oh snot daffleclut to hobble that," said God, "the tooth is sumpty this, and sumpty that and sumpty sumpty else."

"He says that you were consistent," smiled Muckle handing him a goatskin, "and that the truth is sometimes this, and sometimes that and sometimes the other. But you were too tied down to see that. Off you go!"

The next guy didn't have any identity card, the woman who came after him didn't have enough money, and the man after her again didn't have the right measurements. They were all damned. A quiet woman just ahead of us was given the benefit of the doubt because she had nice curly hair and was a distant relation of a nun. She skipped away happily and Adam took three steps up to his judgement.

"Come closer" grunted Muckle, as Adam seemed a little reluctant and not too surprisingly. I was afraid I'd soil my pants when I came next, or else no words would come out of my tongue. My mouth was dry and my lips were cracked and my knees were weak. Adam didn't appear to me to be so frightened but he never was one to let the big occasion get him down. I could see everything perfectly clearly now. The big stream of the damned going off to the left and vanishing down a hole in the ground; the small trickle going off to the right and ascending a shining escalator which appeared to vanish in the blue of the sky. I could also see the face of God and it was clear that he was enjoying every minute of this. There was a permanent smile glued to his face as of somebody wielding power that had never been wielded before. He would take off his glasses every so often but it didn't change the serenity of the smile. If it wasn't this particular day and this particular afternoon that would never come again even the most gloomy person would have to enjoy the balmy sun and the easy warmth.

"Fot is the fie or the fairfore ovoo?" God asked gently, "or waywho war wore rootings, whore poor ants?"

"He is asking you what you have ever done for the environment?" said Muckle, a bit grudgingly.

"I have to admit that I have done nothing at all," said Adam in a kind of a pally way. I thought this was quite inappropriate. "I mean really nothing. And come to think of it I have done nothing either for my neighbours. Or for the state, or for the church, or for the poor, or for the third world. In fact, every single thing I have ever done has been for myself alone. Just me. That's me in a nutshell."

"Well that's it so," said Muckle. "Take yourself off to hell. We have no time here for liars. I know that you once gave a penny to charity when you were a little boy and you could have spent it on sweets. You lied, you bastard! You're not as bad as you make yourself out to be. So fuck off out of my sight." He handed him a mangy-looking goatskin on which there was a large brown stain.

Adam took it from him quietly and was just turning away when I heard the bang. I spun round and saw two holes in God's chest with his life's grace pouring out of them where he had been plugged. I saw the gun in Adam's hand and Muckle drawing the sword from his scabbard. I saw another hole blown in Muckle's skull as he flopped to the ground. I saw the other guards coming with their swords at the ready but they were no match for an automatic pistol. I heard the death-rattle in God's throat as if he was trying to say something to the world as he was leaving it. I wasn't really able to understand them as he never was a very clear speaker. I thought it was something like "Dally the Llama, it is spaghettini" but I couldn't be sure.

"Now that God is dead," Adam said to the world the following day, "we may as well begin all over again. And this time there will be logic and order and justice and peace."

We gave God a good funeral and made sure there was a respectable crowd there. I couldn't attend myself as I was too busy making sense of our new world and was beginning to enjoy the power.

translated by the author

THE GOBSPIEL ACCORDING TO JOHN

Do this; do that; get up; shake yourself; stir your carcass; shift your ass; put on your trousers; pull up your socks; open the door; mind the stranger; give me your plate; eat your dinner; drink your milk; don't eat with your mouth full; hang up your coat; make your bed; be home before dark; sing a song; tell the truth; do your homework; wash the dishes; tidy your room; correct the mistakes; fill in the boxes; watch the water; turn off the television; get the salt; put out the cat; sweep the floor; clean out the car; dress your sister; pay your debts; shut your face; cop on; stay back from the road; reckon the cost; demand your rights; don't forget yourself; keep talking; open your eyes; scrub your teeth; look left and right; keep your mouth closed; cut the grass; hold your piece; help the poor; learn what you can; put it all down to experience; light a candle in the dark; put your right foot forward; take your chance; don't waste your energy; strike the iron when it's hot; keep going; watch your manners; put in the boot; do your duty; squeeze the last ounce; play the game; get stuffed; see what you see; whatever you say say nothing; don't get caught; there will be jam tomorrow; shape up; shake down; get on with it; bugger off; tune up, turn back, drop dead; move right on; fuck your excuses I want my money; say your prayers; it's my party and I'll cry if I want to; if you call me pretty I'll hit you; thou shalt not have strange yobs before me; don't mind him; don't break the law; don't dirty your mouth; don't mumble; don't walk on the flowers; don't lift the child; don't suffer fools gladly; don't take insults lying down; don't wipe your snot on your sleeve; don't go up into the attic; don't go down the garden; don't fall off the tree; don't keep your hands to yourself; don't put your paws in the till; don't say I didn't tell you; don't tell lies; don't funk a fight; don't play dirty; don't lose the match; don't make a pig of yourself; don't quench the candle; don't be like that; don't put your finger in the dyke; don't put the cat in the microwave; don't jump the gun; don't wet your pants; don't ride a bike without a light; don't go without one of them things in your pocket; don't look the other way; don't disembark until the bus stops; don't write on the two sides of the page; don't have it off when you should have it on; don't put your trust in ponces; don't let woebegones be woebegones; don't let them get you; don't get off the bandwagon until the music stops; don't come in here drunk; don't let your meat loaf; don't be in any doubt about it whatsoever, don't put chewing gum on the bedpost overnight; don't forget your contribution on the way out; don't throw your granny off the bus, don't hit the nail with your head; don't do that again or I'll put your teeth out through your arse; don't worship false gods.

Well I have to say that he had it coming the bastard he deserved it from the moment he laid the strap on my hand the weak-faced wimp even though it was marsbars and i.q. who brought the frog into the class he blamed me completely who does he think he is the poop or something and he nearly took the skin from my hands the nerd but that wasn't the worst of it o no it wasn't but the leer he had from ear to ear the craphead as if he was getting pleasure from it the born-again asshole after he telling us we shouldn't get pleasure from anything and that we shouldn't go behind the shed with the big boys on the way home the whore's git and he'd have another kind of leer on his snout as he told us and we'd see his tobacco-stained teeth the dick-head and the big gash down the middle of his tongue like the rift-valley he beat us to know so he did herr haemorrhoid but marsbars and i.q. were over the moon when they heard of the revenge I had planned this time the fucker not like the last time when we wrapped up the lumpa shit in the pretty box and festooned it with christmas ribbons the coprophagous cunt and sent it to him by registered post so that he would get it with his breakfast of greasy sausages and hairy bacon the pedagogic piss-pot and we were the ones grinning from our elbe to our euphrates that morning as he tried to the rectal rambo think of the latin verbs turdo turdas turdat he was one page ahead of us in the book but this time we were determined to go the whole hog the zapped-out zeroid just to show that low-life forms like him or like he couldn't get away with it the bumbo because we knew it was our duty not to let teachers or parents ride roughshod over us on account of our dignity like and as killing is the ultimate organism we said why not as with i.q.'s deep voice and he being a good actor and all as well as being a good forger we used to get him to write our parents' notes that we were sick or visiting the dentist or that our aunt down the country died and so that girl in the newspaper office didn't suspect anything when he told her between sobs that his father had snuffed it had kicked the slop-bucket had pissed away had gone to his beloved sleep had shipped it quietly had gone to his eternal sward had put out the flame was now as good as the door-nails he hammered and he was dearly beloved of and much regretted by his dear wife and children and that the remains would leave The Church of Perpetual Suckers at five o'clock and they could send the bill to him as the eldest son the fart-faggot and I don't think he ever understood the grin on our faces even when the leather was hopping off our hands because it was nothing compared with the leer on our backsides because we knew in our heart of hearts and from our history lessons and from the TV that there was no revenge as sweet as death the bed-messer but we only regretted we didn't see his face or his wife's when they read of his death the vindictive vasectomized vamper for we were the boys for him and his prolapsed pile I'm telling you the old shitfaced bollocky bastard.

Slow romantic music in the background. Sugary-sweet singing coming from a singer off-stage. Dim lights. Young ladies in their teens on the left. They are examining themselves and one another with some expectation. A young man enters from the right and approaches them.

JOHN (*well-manneredly*): May I have the pleasure of the next dance with you, please?

TALL GIRL (*looking at him disdainfully*): Hmrlfx!

(*She turns away and retreats into the crowd.*)

JOHN (*out loud*): Sorry, I didn't know you were pregnant!

(*Trying another one*) Would you care to dance?

BRUNETTE: With you? (*Nose up, chin out, baring her teeth*) Do you think I'm nuts or something?

JOHN: Sorry, I didn't know you were gay! (*Walks down the line of girls.*) Shake the floor will we?

REDHEAD (*stiffly*): I'm not dancing.

JOHN: Sorry, I didn't know you had BO! (*Tries another*) What about you, hah? Are you coming? (*She says nothing but follows him out onto the floor centre-stage*)

BLONDE (*chewing gum*): Are you into Elphin Grot?

JOHN: They're OK. But they're not as good as Celtic Phlegm, I think.

BLONDE: I wouldn't call that thinking. Nobody's as good as Elphin Grot. At least they live up to their reputation.

JOHN: And you should know?

BLONDE (*emphatically*): I know everything.

They don't say anything for a while but John snuggles in closely to her as the music gets softer and slower.

JOHN (*speaking into her ear*): Do you have an apartment or did you come with a friend?

BLONDE (*into his ear also*): Did you have cabbage for your dinner?

JOHN (*puzzled*): Not as far as I know. Why do you ask?

BLONDE: I just thought I felt the stump.

And on the sixth day it came to pass that there was a game in the Field and John was there. And the other boys were invited also unto the game. And the manager was there before them with anger on his countenance. And he said unto them: What is it to thee or to me if you foul forty yards out from the goal. For I say unto you that a point on the score-board is better than a goal in your net. And he ordained them to listen carefully unto him because they were like sheep without a shepherd and he began to instruct them that what was highly esteemed among men was an abomination in his sight. But he saw the cowardice in them and he said: whosoever amongst you hath a hurley also hath a hatchet, and he who hath a hatchet is able to cut down the fig tree of the enemy. For what doth it profit a man to win all the balls and to lose the game itself. And he sighed inwardly in his spirit for he knew that they were no bloody good. And the multitudes came from the two parishes unto them and they laid their cloaks upon the grass and some amongst them even did open their umbrellas as that was the kind of day it was and those who were first and those who were last and those who were on both sides were shouting and roaring and making whoopee and hosannas. And when half-time came he was still angry and the red was in his cheeks and he lifted up his eyes and he charged them saying: O you brutes of vipers, give an account of your stewardship. For how long will I have to suffer thus? He who hath ears to hear let him hear. And he spoke to them in plain bad language so that they might understand. Take heed to yourselves. Gird your lines for the winning of all is within you. Remember your wives' lot for even thus shall it be on the day of reckoning. It is impossible but that offences will come; but woe unto him through whom they come. Between us and them there is a great gulf fixed so that they who pass to them are guilty of the abomination of execration. For verily I say unto you, this kind can be driven forth by nothing but by flailing and hacking. For he who has much, more will be given unto him and he who has nothing will be taken off the field. These things I have told you so that you would not be scandalized. He who is to be floored, floor him, and he who is to be split, split him, and he who is not with you is against you. And I have many more things to tell you which I cannot say now. But he sent them away and charged them straight away not to disclose any part of the advice he had given them. But John knew well what had to be done and he looked at them and said: Follow me. And when he had taken the legs from under his opponent the third time and had smote him upon the right ear the referee called unto him and said: Dost thou not know that it is written that thou shalt not bear false evidence against thine opposing player? And he denied it and said: I know not what thou sayest. But he began to curse and to swear, saying, I know not this man of whom you speak. Why askest thou me? I laid neither leg nor stick on him. But the referee sent him forth from the field so that the strictures would be fulfilled that a bone of them should not be broken. But he understood not what had been said and the meaning was hidden from him. And when the chief cheese and the elders sat down to discuss his case they suspended him for six months and he went off alone unto the mountain to throw his guts up.

HATCHETMAN, WHAT OF THE NIGHT?
So then the night is dark and the air is black and the wood is creaking, the bats are abroad hunting the blue moon, the sailors are drinking, the cat is chewing its fur, the horse is in the field yawning metaphorically,

powder with a woman inside it is stalking the streets, the thief is waiting
her chance, the yuppie is yuppieing in the night club, the priest is thinking
of the great sins of the past, the waves are saying farewell to the wind,
the international terrorist is tending his bomb, the teacher is tetchy, the
painted lady is pounding the pavement, the cars are smoking their pipes,
the rust is doing its worst on the broaches of breasts, the pig's tail is
curling its wee, the contaminated water is waiting in the taps for the
morning, the window-blind is swallowing the shadows, the gooseberry
bushes are sticking out their tongues at the garden, the child is teaching
wisdom to the psychologist, the lamb is lying down with the lion but is
keeping his options open, the stairs is on the way up, the train is setting
the night on fire, the seal is blowing his nose on the beach, the clouds
are bustle pinching the mountains, the flashes of inspiration are leaving
people's heads, the children have at last shut up, the sidewalks are
beginning to stir, wisdom is gathering in the brains of fools, trees are
wrestling with the stars, cats are howling on their beat, whorls of sleep
are coming in on the west wind, somebody out there is dying, somebody
out there is knitting the garment of horror, somebody out there is
smashing his car, somebody out there is kissing a lamp-post, somebody
out there is spreading dew on the grass, somebody out there is turning
candles in the dark, somebody out there is making sandwiches for the
morning, somebody out there is trying to read Freud, somebody out there
is putting salt in the buttermilk, somebody out there frankly doesn't give
a damn, somebody out there is murdering the Musak, this young man
knows what he's made of, this young man has the right stuff, this young
man is acting the mick, this young man is doodling the dandy, this young
man is hugging the mugger, this young man is kneading the dough, this
young man is plucking the fig, this young man is tapping the column,
this young man is stirring the stew, this young man is flaking the flint,
this young man is venting the venison, this young man is besting the
beaver, this young man is hauling the ashes, this young man is dunking
the pumpkin, this young man is honking the donkey, this young man
is tooting the rootie, this young man is happening the stance, this young
man is wobbling the colly, this young man is jollying the roger, this young
man is humouring the hubris, this young man is porking the beans, this

young man is burning the bush, this young man is abrogating the absolute, this young man is reintegrating himself with the basic stuff of the universe, this young man has the poof of the pudding, this young man has had enough, this young man is going asleep.

A fine young man he was, so he was, and he went off to earn his keep as I will tell you know. He was going off now and always and was getting no good of it at all until he came to this club as the dark twilight of night was coming down. It was the last of the day then and there was neither soul nor sinner in the club, so he thought. And so he betook himself into the back room and who should he meet there but three fine women on whom he pitched his fancy. He asked them was there any chance of a bit of sport or what or could he stop the night until the morrow. They told him that there was not indeed to be sure and to be off with himself and to make out somewhere else and to be annoying other bodies. He was a distance from the club and the black of night upon him when he met another woman.

"Isn't it late you're out gallivanting?" he said to the woman. "Were you in that club down there below?" he said.

"I was," she said.

"Who was before you within?" he said.

"There were some men," she said.

"And they wouldn't give you lodgings for the night?" he said.

"They would not," he said.

"Nor me neither," says he, he said.

"Success and benison to you for you're one after my own art," she said. "Come along you blasted man and maybe you'll get lodgings for the night yet."

Well and good. They rose and bestirred themselves and went on their way. And when they were a while along the road there was nobody for them to see and nothing for them to notice only fine tall mansions with big gardens and fancy cars which would gladden your heart. They did not stop nor shorten the journey until they came to a neat cottage beside the road. Anyway they went in and she put down a big pot of stew and a big pot of potatoes to boil.

"Ah well, upon my soul," said the woman, "sit down or do something useful."

"It's early days yet," he said, "to be stopping the night."
"There is no man the likes of you who passes this way that I do not keep for the duration of the whole night," she said.

Well then! He took off his coat anyway. She had a big fire blazing and she produced a pack of cards.
"Will you play a game with me?" she said.
"I will why not," he said.
They started to play, herself and himself, and when they did she won the game against him at the very first go.
"Aha," she said, "I put as a judgement and binding spells on you, and under the great displeasure of the year not to eat two meals at the same table nor to sleep twice on one bed until you do the job with me!" she said.
Well then this was bad news for him but it is as well for me to shorten the story. Well he rose up with a leap and they went at it hammer and tongues, sally and forth, blazes and boiling, curry and fervour, cods and wallop, box and cox, derry and down, nonny and know, lute and nail, snatch and berry, milk and cunny, rump and stake, peak and boo, rod and sinker, smullet and stern, rattle and roll, storm and drang, hokey and pokey, gammon and baking, what and knot, jimmy and joys, willie and sing, whoops and daisy, dick and cavet, jackall and hide, fan and winkle, hock and pintle, whole and shebang, needle and anchor, frankly and further, knead and gnashing, hairs and aces, yin and yang, excal and burr, gung and ho, yank and oodle, cannon and ball, bracket and hinge, amoor and priap, mills and boom, jigerry poker crackling baloney tickula tickulorum for ovur and ovum onan.
"Well that's over now and anyhow, my man above," she said. "You must marry me now," she said, "that's the law of the land. Are you willing?" she said.
Well and good and not otherwise and he gave her a long look.
"Wisha, is that the way it is?" he said, rubbing a palm to his eyes, to his forelock, to his brows. "Well," he said, the young man said, "that's

not bad at all, by dad. What I want is what you want as long as the day rises on the morrow and the sap rises in the marrow."

And it is what she said, "Here," she said, "take that for now," throwing him his clothes. "Great stuff and God's greeting to you," she said, "we'll be knocking good times out of the hard times for many times to come."

It is reported that is how John married the red woman and it was said that they were often seen abroad among the cocks of hay making their sport for themselves in joy and happiness.

And that's a true story without any lie, you know!

WHAT DID HE LEARN IN THE COURSE OF HIS LIFE?
He learned that he was nobody's fool, that money opened all doors, that speech is the mother of troubles, that the house of bondage had many whips, that a small still voice is never heard, that out of the mouths of babes and sucklings comes forth dribble, that two and two made four sometimes, that the writing on the wall was never clear, that there was not much beyond wit's end, that he that spareth the rod has no sons, that the philosophic pill gilded nothing, that between the candy store on the corner and the chapel on the hill there was a lot of corn, that blue was the colour of his true love's hair in the morning, that there were many good reasons for doing nothing, that the long finger was better than a thumb, that the sheikhs shall inherit the earth, that those who go down to the sea in ships are usually sailors, that the whores of wood had drawers of water, that one should give a lie for a lie and a truth for a truth, that whereof one cannot speak one is obliged to bullshit, that the only way out was back, that the answer was blowing in the wind, that it was always dirty on the pig's back, that the ball was the name of the game, that a radical chic goes to the root of things, that the delta of venus demanded a lot of tributes, that the fool on the hill watches over all, that he didn't like Mondays, that coke was the real thing, that a friend indeed was a friend with speed, that the ogres of thought were not as effective as the curses of obstruction, that raw data tastes best when cooked, that most pottery is a heinous sham, that going to the wall doesn't mean you have to wail about it, that now is sooner than then, that the Great Architect never got a degree, that it was difficult to swing on the

roundabouts, that the tooth doesn't always out, that to be or not to be isn't even a question, that he who dares sins, that every slip is Freudian that every tom and dick is hairy, that smart cookies don't crumble, that a wild-goose chase sometimes caught a white elephant, that it was easier to fly than to stay up, that hush puppies rarely bark, that forked fingers were more feared than forked tongues, that screwball was a kind of cocktail, that a bird in the hand meant none in the bush, that walking the plank meant you made a big splash, that farce was better than force, that the brodingnag wasn't half as bad as the bob-tailed nag, that insultants should earn more than consultants, that you couldn't squeeze the lemon out of lemonade, that his gun was for hire even if he was only dancing in the dark, that lust we are and unto lust we always turn, that hard cheese was a tough titty, that the flighty are often callen, that crabbed sages and truth don't always go together, that life was a hard slut to crack, that there was no rule like misrule, that nobody mattered diddly-squat and that everything was a long way up the creek and past turning.

Other things he did also which made his spirit leap,
The flight of owls whom he feared from within the deep
Where all the ladders start in the old tack and toe slop
Of his parts; these he exorcized and got
A new cheap toy lamp that gave little light
But loved the signs, the embranglement that tried
To dismember the dully sober from the wildly fue
And showed this from that betimes in our antediluvian zoo.
So hoyted he upfront down-market between the shots
While others wavered between the profit and the loss
That his soul purpled itself on carls of turd
While others lived the beefy breathing of the herds,
And scobberlotchery became a kind of loam
Wherein the calm empire of a happy soul
Was thrunged with sense and hate and love and howls and peace
That the unpurged images of day were forced to recede
Before the cobbled force of all those and them and that
The monstrous regiment of Being and All This Crap and Fact.

"So raise the roof beams high, you team of carpenters
And forget the fears of ancient harbingers!"
The cry is me, and mine, and member and *même chose*
And ourselves and us and all we have is ours,
For in and out, about, above and below
It is always the same old stupid asshole show,
And for all the priests and goodmen and sages say
Their nutritious images only choke the simple way
From hand to mouth and the other orifices given
Whose ordures we must, our luck, just do their bidding.
So that's it then, have fun, be good, what's new?
I'm me myself, but for fuck's sake, who are you?

Here then are your crutches, here then is your rocking-chair, here is your cup of tea, here is your sugar daddy, here are your sleeping-tablets, here is your mug of milk, here is your knee blanket, here are your soft slippers, here is your television programme, here is your glass of water, here is your plate of porridge, here is your bed pot, here is your scrambled egg, here is your wedge and thin edge, here is your black ticket, here is your red penny, here is your woolly fold, here is your pipe and tobacco, here is your jolly grog, here is your faithful old dog, here are your strong glasses, here is your same old tune, here is your purple hanky, here are your false teeth, here are your muffs and your miffs, here is your photo album, here is your empty gun, here is your fur coat, here is your buttwipe, here is your long john, here are your heavy boots, here is the pale horse, here is the bottom line, here is the endgame, here is the candle to light you to bed, this is the stairs up, this is the open door, this is the beddy ready, this is the pillow of dreams, this is the rich doctor, this is the magic bottle, this is the lay of lays, no that is not an angel, this is your parting shot, this is your big jump, this is the final curtain, that is only a shadow, this is the man with the scythe, do you hear the plug being pulled, that is a buzz in your ears, that is the hand that slipped, that is the beautiful memory, that is the way of all trash, that is your bier and casket, that's about it.

translated by the author

THE LAST BUTTERFLY

It was my last summer before I went to secondary school. If it wasn't, it was certainly the last summer I spent with my brother as the following year he went off to work in Tramore on the roundabouts. We were staying with my aunt at Coolfeakle and she was as changeable as the clouds. But she did let us wander at will through the fields and meadows as long as we fetched water from the well. I thought she kept a cobweb on her head until Martin told me it was a hair-net she wore to keep her hair from going grey. I never knew when he was joking me or not.

We had picked mushrooms in the morning because it had been damp, and Aunty fried them with buttered potatoes and cabbage for dinner. They were things I would never eat at home but hours rambling through the fields with the wind at my back and the grass under my feet would give you an appetite for old boots. The sun came out while we ate and I could see Aunty smile at it as if she knew something that it did not.

"Not before time, either," she said, as she shuffled back to the dresser for a side-plate.

"I suppose it'll shine all the time after tomorrow," Martin said. "Just after we get the train."

"And it'll blaze when we go back to school," I chimed in, showing I could be as pessimistic as the rest.

"Don't moan," Aunty said, but not severely. "Moaning never stopped the rain. Did you never hear that?"

We didn't answer as we didn't want another long gabble about the weather. It amazed me how grown-ups could go on and on and on about the weather as if it really mattered. My motto was if you didn't like the weather just wait a while and it would change.

"I think I'll catch ladybirds," I said after we had put our dishes in the basin, but I didn't get any great response from Martin.

He came with me none the less. We went through the Potter's field and up past the Bracken Glen and round by Maggie Maurice's old house which was now deserted since she was taken away and out as far as

Aughinish. We could see the sea from there sucking the gentle heat from the sun and rolling round the rocks to the shore. I hadn't caught any ladybirds yet but I still had my jamjar.

A fly went by with a hum in it but who wants to catch a fly? Martin said,"This is boring."

I didn't think so because I liked the sea and the sky and the green fields that were everywhere and laid themselves out in all directions. Sometimes I wished I could just run and run and run away over the horizon and throw kisses at the wheat and the corn and smell everything as it is first thing in the morning. There were times when I would love to be a scarecrow but that was a secret I would never tell anybody.

"Look, look at them," Martin said, grabbing me by the arm and pointing my eyes towards Muckers' Acre.

I didn't see anything unusual but Martin seemed intent on showing me anyway. There was the field and some haystacks and a man and another person near the gate. He was wearing a bright red and yellow anorak which reminded me of fried eggs and tomato ketchup. His size shadowed the other person and it wasn't until they began to climb over the gate that I saw it was a woman. She wore a green headscarf the colour of cooking apples of the kind that are too bitter for even Aunty's tarts.

"Come on, let's follow them," Martin said.

"What for?"

"It might be fun."

"I want to collect ladybirds."

"You're a sissy."

"You're silly."

"Maybe they're spies."

"There's nothing round here to spy on."

"O yes there is. The Relihan's house was broken into last week and they know it was sussed out first. I bet you that's what they're up to. Why else would they be going through the fields and not round by the road?"

I couldn't answer that so I tagged on behind. Martin kicked the thistles as if they were footballs but I preferred to leave them standing. Anyway, most of them just jumped back up as if he was wasting his time.

I thought time was there to be wasted but Martin was the one who always wanted to be doing something. We stayed at least a field behind and they were making very slow progress. Maybe they were noticing everything like Martin said as spies and robbers have to notice everything. We also had to stay out of sight and picked and ate some blackberries from the bushes. I wouldn't let him use my jar to collect them as I detested blackberry jam and I knew what I wanted it for.

"Think Aunty will kill us if we come home with our feet wet?" I asked, as we were going through a soggy dip towards a stream.

"Who cares?" Martin said. "We're going home tomorrow. Ma won't mind. She'll be washing all our clothes anyhow."

"I like it here," I said. "I think I'd like to live in the country when I grow up. It's big. It's wild."

"It's boring."

Martin thought everything was boring apart from his crummy records. He'd listen to the same song for hours and discuss it with his pals. I think Ma sent him down the country just for a bit of peace.

We were trailing along beside the stream on the way to Berwick's Wood when I saw it.

It floated out from underneath a tall fern and moved on to a ray of sunlight. It had the most beautiful black wings I had ever seen and they were tinged with red like jam through a doughnut.

I could not tell one kind of butterfly from another but I knew that this one was special. It flitted in and out of the sunlight as if it was preening itself and more than anything else in the world I just wanted to stay in that spot and admire it.

"Look, Martin! Look!" I whispered, fearing that any loud voice would frighten it away.

Martin looked back and cast one eye on it. "Yes, it's a butterfly or a moth or something. It's lovely. Now come on."

"Just a minute," I said, "I want to look at it."

It moved across the stream as if on a ferry of sundust and just as I was about to wave it goodbye it alighted on a thin reed which jutted out from the bank. It appeared even more beautiful when at rest and I stepped out onto the stones to get a closer look.

I could not believe my luck when it didn't fly away. I stretched out my hand breathlessly and yet it did not move. The black was lovely, lovely like the mouth of a cave and the red was as the dawn coming through it. I could have prayed that it would never move and that I could stay there watching it more beautiful than all its surroundings for ever.

I heard Martin shouting at me from up the stream. He seemed miles away but somehow I didn't care. He shouted again more angrily this time and I knew I would have to leave. Quickly, without thinking I stretched out the jamjar and enclosed my butterfly under the lid. Thankfully he could make no sound as I did not wish to hurt it in any way and I knew that I would soon let it go.

"Hurry up! What's keeping you? We've lost them."

I tried to show him my black beauty but he wasn't interested. He just kept pushing ahead through the scrub and yapping at me to move it.

"Damn it," he said as our rough path forked out from the edge of the stream towards the wood. "Because of you we'll never know which way they went. You've blown it."

"Maybe they left a clue," I said, hoping I might have said the right thing. "Maybe we'll find a piece of cloth on a bush."

"Rubbish," he said, pushing ahead. "We'll just have to go one way and take a chance we're right."

I followed him faithfully through the wood even pretending to hide behind the same trees as he did. Every so often I got a chance to look at my butterfly and he would gently flit his wings at me. The brambles that coiled out to ambush us didn't seem to bother Martin and I wouldn't have minded if he didn't let them snap back on me. I don't think he even noticed.

We had been walking up a hill for some time when the trees began to thin out. We came to a barbed wire fence but the path turned and ran along beside it. There were very few trees on the other side of the fence and Martin said we should go through as we would get a better view and might spot them. We moved further along the path to try to find an opening when I saw the green scarf caught on the wire.

"Come on," Martin urged, and I went through first and then held the wire up for him as he was bigger.

We ran along the grass margin of the trees and then up the hill again as if we were on a murder hunt. I'm not sure where we went after that as I just followed Martin as he ran and crouched and zigzagged and ducked through ferns and bushes until we came to the lane.

"I hope this leads on to the road," I said. "I'm tired."

"Come on," he said, and I followed.

The lane ran right up to a high wall with a big wooden door cold in the middle. It was closed. We pushed but it would not open.

"What do we do now," I said, "go all the way back?"

"Give me a leg up," Martin said, as he tried to get a foothold in the wall. I helped him and he managed to hoist himself up far enough to see over.

"What is it?" I asked, "what's there?"

"Nothing much only another big field."

"Well come on then."

"Just a minute. I'll be down in a minute."

"Give me a hand up so."

"There's no need. It's nothing. Just a field."

"Must be a great view if you ask me."

When he did come down I thought he was angry with me. He said nothing for a while but just strode away back towards the hill which seemed much higher now. I found it more difficult to keep up with him this time and I knew it was a long way home.

"What's that you have in the jar?" he asked, suddenly.

"It's my butterfly," I said. "Don't you remember?"

"Show it to me."

He glanced at it briefly and what looked like a smile appeared on his lips.

"Silly girlish stuff," he sneered, as he opened the jamjar and rolled my beautiful black butterfly between the palms of his hands.

All I ever remembered then was the black powder falling and the fleck of red on his fingernails.

translated by the author

FABLES

THE TROUBLESOME YOUNG WOMAN

There was once a troublesome young woman whom her parents called a little bitch. Others called her other things but as her parents loved her dearly it was enough to call her a little bitch. And because they loved her dearly they did not throw her on the street even when she constantly stole their credit cards, crashed her mother's car, ripped her father's clothes, called them stupid fucking wrinklies and acted the general, well, bitch. But because they loved her dearly they would do anything to help her and even went so far as to bring her to a psychiatrist.

"It's penis-envy," he said, "no doubt about it. I've seen it many times before. Young women her age all suffer from it even if they don't admit it. And just because they don't admit it doesn't mean they don't suffer from it. Nothing here that a good man and a good bit of bonking will not cure."

Because they loved her and because they were paying good money to the psychiatrist they let her out about the town with as much money to visit the best night-clubs and stay in the best hotels as she wanted. Not that she needed any urging nor advice about where to go. But it was nice to be able to do it with her parents' (and the psychiatrist's) permission.

She had a ball of a time with big hunky macho muscular types and long wiry athletic fit-freaks and flashy moneyed long-practised swingers for as long as she could and wanted. After that she came home and put the cat in the microwave oven, cut the heads off all the roses, gouged the tyres of her daddy's car, pissed in her mother's swimming pool and generally acted the, well, bitch.

Because they loved her and were paying good money they brought her back to the psychiatrist.

"It wasn't penis-envy," said her father without going into much detail, "of that we can be absolutely sure."

"Well if it wasn't penis-envy," said the psychiatrist, "it must be something else. Wait till I see."

And he took a big leatherbound book down from the shelf.

WHAT IS TO BE DONE?
[from the play *Tagann Godot/Godot Turns Up*]

There was this man once upon a time and he was very confused. He searched through the libraries of the world and the scrolls of the scribes but he got no answer. And he studied with the wise professors of learning in the best institutions of knowledge and got no answer. And he starved himself for forty days and nights and even took little pinches of mescaline to open the doors of perception but still he did not get the answer he desired.

So he decided to go on his way and walk from the top of the world to the bottom of the world in order to see could he meet anyone who might answer his question.

And on his way he met an important rich man with money-bags under his eyes and with golden threads through his hair. And he asked of him gently and with proper manners, "Kind sir", he said, "you are a man of the world. You go here, there, and everywhere. You breakfast in London and dine in Montevideo. You have enough money to break the bank at Monte Carlo or to play footsie with the stock exchange. Would you mind telling me, please, what this is all about, what is the meaning of life?"

And he looked into the eyes of the rich man and he saw the money dancing in them.

And the rich man said to him as he might say to his underlings: "Sorry boy. Go away. I am too busy. I have to buy another bank. And anyway, it's a stupid question."

And when he left the place he heard the rich man laugh, and his laugh shook the ground beneath his feet.

And after that he went to the palace of the King. The King was within perusing a map under eyebrows that looked like moving forests. His fingernails curled like dragons on his abacus as he counted his soldiers. And as he perused with pleasure his forehead took on the contours of an unconquered country and his teeth glistened like burnished shields.

And the man asked him with suitable obsequiousness but in all honesty, "Your most worthy and inestimable excellency," he said, "you are the ruler of many kingdoms. You say to men come and they come, and go to war and they go to war. There is nobody but that does not bow down before your might and majesty and do your bidding. Please, please tell me, what this is all about, what is the meaning of life?"

And he looked into the depths of the eyes of the king and he saw power dancing within.

And the King said to him with suitable royal impatience: "Begone from here, you fool, before I chop off your head. Don't you see that I am too busy erecting monuments and defeating knavish enemies? And anyway, it is a stupid question."

And when he left that place he could hear the King and his courtiers laughing and their laughs echoed like trampling hooves on the flagstones of the road.

And after that he went to the Temple. The Chief Priest was within praying on his bended knees. And the man spoke to him and said: "Your most benign grace and utmost holiness," he said, "you have read all the books of theology and the scrolls of scripture. You know the lives of the saints and the prognostications of the prophets. You offer sacrifices and make obeisances daily. You fast and abstain. You keep the ten commandments and possess the seven gifts of the holy ghost and practise the cardinal virtues. Can you please, please, tell me what this is all about, what is the meaning of life?"

And he peered down deeply into the eyes of the Chief Priest and he saw sanctity and holiness dancing madly in them.

And the Chief Priest said to him with authority: "Depart from me before I set the faithful upon you. Dost thou not see that I am too busy adoring God? I have to make reparations for the sins of the world. And anyway, it is a stupid question."

And when he left that place with a troubled heart he heard the Chief Priest laughing, and his laugh drew echoes down from the speedwell blue of the sky.

And outside of the Temple he saw a small boy begging.

"Help me," said the boy, "I have had nothing to drink for three days and I am dying of thirst."

And when the man saw the wretchedness of the boy he cried bitterly.

And he filled a cup with his tears and he gave it to the boy and the boy drank it and was grateful.

And now I ask you, which of these people did most good, the men who laughed, or the man who cried?

THE STORY-TELLER

Once upon a time and a very long time ago there was a story-teller who came from out of the east telling stories. He would stop people in the street, grab them by the sleeve and whisper coarsely in their ear, "Hey, did you hear the one about . . .?"

They didn't take much notice of him at first because they thought him odd, and peculiar, and even a little queer. He also had a rough country accent as if he hadn't quite taken the potato out of his mouth. In truth, he was a bit of a hayseed. How could anyone who told stories on street corners or in the fields or in the back rooms of pubs be taken seriously?

But gradually he became a bit of a cult figure. Among a minority of like-minded bumpkins at first, people who enjoyed tales about country life, and sowing seeds, and harvesting apples and going to school through the fields. But when he then started on the stories about whores and prostitutes more of the spivs and the slickers pricked up their ears. He had some pretty good yarns about youths getting pissed and indulging in great bouts of debauchery in the big city as soon as they escaped from the farm.

He also said some weird things that didn't make much sense but people remembered them because they were catchy and way-out. "If you ever throw a party," he said once at the end of a story, as these bits were often attached to the main telling, "if you ever throw a party like the fat capitalist in my tale, remember to invite everybody – the poor, the hoboes, the junkies, the scumbags on the streets, god-dam filthy immigrants, crapartists of every colour, journalists, hustlers, the blind, the lame and the maimed. Do it this way 'cause they can never invite you back."

He was quick with the paradox and the quip when people tried to heckle him although he did lose his cool once or twice and fell back on calling people who didn't fancy his stories "hypocrites" and "shite-hawks." Maybe it was because of this that people began to get a bit cheesed off. Or maybe it was the sheer banality of weighty statements like "Look, peace is inside you and peace is outside you" or stories that said you should be happy with whatever miserable pittance a boss gave you. More than that, however, it was maybe just that fashions change and maybe he began to run out of stories.

In his latter years when he would start on some yarn some wag would shout "Heard it before!" from the street corner, or murmurs of "Boring, boring," would come from those who expected more, or "Why don't you tell us a true story, about real life?" from those who didn't like folklore. There was also a rumour that all the story-tellers were to be banished as they were not conducive to good citizenship and that society needed skills that were really useful and practical and economically relevant and market-driven.

Nobody was too surprised when his body was discovered in the hills above the city. It only made a brief mention in the evening papers because of the grass and pebbles that were stuffed in his mouth as if somebody was making the point that he should be shut up.

The funny thing was that people began telling his stories again shortly after his murder. Somebody said it was a good career-move. And others began to make up stories about him. And others began to make up stories about the stories. And yet others a commentary on the stories. And yet others again an exegesis of the commentary on the stories. And later an explanation of the exegesis of the commentary on the stories. And then an analysis of the explanation of the exegesis of the commentary on the stories. And then a critique of the analysis of the explanation of the exegesis of the commentary on the stories.

And then somebody remembered that the story-teller himself once said, "Look, a story is just like a mustard seed . . ."

THE SINGER AND THE SONG

The chief wizard of the one and only true faith was much loved and highly regarded. He travelled the world in his golden plane and kissed the ground in humility and thanksgiving when he landed safely. He shook hands with the great and mighty with their baby-seal-lined gloves and waved at the poor and lonely who gawped on the balconies.

High or mighty, poor or lowly, they all loved his words of wisdom. Money flowed in – even when he didn't ask for it – after a particularly good television appearance. Cheque-books and purses and wallets and bank accounts were opened as quickly as any poor person might say "God help me" or "Why doesn't God help me?" Rich and good people loved him, and kings and emperors adored him, and presidents of rich countries whose people were fat and forgetful slobbered over his sweet and beautiful words.

"Love the poor," he would say with a kind of sincerity that could not be denied, "but remember the poor you will have with you always."

"Love justice and righteousness," he would say solemnly through his loudspeaker to the crowd, "but remember to render unto Caesar the things that are Caesar's and anything else after that isn't God's."

"Don't love worldly things," he might say, "but remember that the labourer is worthy of his hire and never refuse what is rightly yours and earned by the sweat of your brow or any other kind of sweat."

These were the kind of words that showed that God was in his Heaven and all was well with the world – at least in the northern hemisphere or where geographers called "The First World".

One day, however, he changed his tune. He did this suddenly without any warning. There was no easy explanation for this and even psychobiographers were baffled. It might have been sunstroke the more literal tried to explain, or a kick from a horse, or a nightmare or even just one of those things. It was as if the conditional clause was excised from his brain by a form of grammatical circumcision.

"Sell all you have and give it to the poor," he would say without pause or hesitation.

"Justice and whatever is right even if the sky falls," he would say and stop with a full stop as big as a library.

"Don't kill. Don't steal. Don't fornicate. Don't curse." He would say this as if it was the most natural thing in the world and if he had been saying it for years.

"Pay no heed for tomorrow. Do not save or store. Look at the swallows. They neither reap nor sow and yet God minds them. Live for today. Love everybody even if they fuck you up." You know the kind of stuff.

So it wasn't any surprise when they started to abandon him.

Some threatened the law. Others hanging or thumbscrews. Others said it was blasphemy. Others said he should be stoned if he wasn't already.

He had to escape in the middle of the night and retreat to the desert where truth was either wet or dry.

"Now, I know," he said while he spoke to the stones in his cave, "I always thought that they loved me. But it appears that they only loved the nice things that I said."

PROGRESS

There was a perfectly happy man who lived underneath a tree. He ate the fruit and the nuts that fell often and in abundance into his lap. He was never hungry.

He never had to stir a limb nor shake a leg nor wiggle an extremity except when he had to answer the call of nature.

One day a student came his way. He was studying business and entrepreneurship in the University of Limerick and walked with a swagger as if he was a Cork hurler.

"Look," he said to the lazy dosser underneath the tree, "look at the great and wonderful opportunity you are missing to make money and get on in the world. Instead of eating this fruit and chewing these nuts why don't you collect them all together and sell them to the shops, or at the market, or at the fair? Or even better than that, why don't you plant some of them in the ground so that other trees might grow, and more fruit would fall, and greater nuts will come, and you should make an even bigger and fatter profit?"

"And why would I want to do that?" said the lazy man under the tree out of a half-closed eye.

"So that you would make money, of course."

"And why would I want to make money?"

Even though the student from the University of Limerick didn't really understand the question he tried to answer it as best he could because the education which he had received hadn't quite erased or banished the good manners which he naturally possessed.

"Well," he said, said the student, "if you had enough money you could do anything at all you liked. Maybe, even, you wouldn't have to do any thing at all. You could be idle all day long. You could rest and take it easy."

"And what do you think I am doing now?" asked the man who lived under the tree.

GREATER LOVE THAN THIS

When they told Pat's wife that he was dead she cried until she could cry no more. She dressed herself in black clothes and she tore her hair from its roots. She cried again even though her eyes were dry and could give no more water.

Those dry white tears fell on her scoured cheeks. She spoke dark and heartbroken words to all who came near her. She could not open her ears to words of charity or consolation.

They laid her husband's body out in the bed and she spoke sweet and sorrowful words to him between bouts of wailing and screaming. She did not sleep that first night, nor the second.

Every waking minute they had spent together rushed through her mind, all the joy and the happiness and the love they had shared ended in this cold shroud.

She threw herself on his body while he lay on the bed. She kissed him passionately on his cold, cold lips while he lay in his coffin. She would not let them put the lid on it until they had no choice, and even then they couldn't secure it.

She was dragged screaming into the funeral car on the day of the burial. She nearly died of grief every inch of the way to the graveyard. Greater love than this no woman ever had for a man, nor any wife for a husband.

When they lowered the coffin into the grave she let out a piercing cry which reached up to Heaven and tore down deep into the earth.

And while she did not succeed in throwing herself into that black hole after her husband's coffin she ensured that it was filled with beautiful flowers rather than with clay. Thousands and thousands and thousands of flowers and wreaths and bouquets of every colour and smell were piled into that grave wherein her husband was laid.

But when Pat woke up in his coffin some short time later he realized he wasn't in his own bed. He raised the lid of the coffin just a fraction and his nose was filled with the sweet and fragrant smell of flowers. But he could not lift it any further because of the heavy weight of love pressing him down.

FLAT EARTH

In those far off days when people were a lot less gullible than they are now some people maintained that the earth was as flat as a billiard-table. They said that if you went to the edge of the world you would fall off and go down, down, down – to hell, maybe, or certainly to the Kingdom of Darkness from which there was no return.

But there were others who said that the world was as round as a ball and that if you walked west you would certainly return from the east, no different from a fly doddling around an apple.

But there were others who said that the world was oval-shaped, but nobody bothered with them as anybody who played with oval balls was *ipso facto* a bit queer.

But those who maintained that the world was flat like a billiard-table soon began to fight with those who thought it was round and circular like a ball. And even though there were wise men and elders and even geniuses on each side they could not agree whether the flatters or the ballers were ultimately right as they had no common ground between them.

And because they were people, and because they couldn't possibly think of any other way of resolving their conflict, and because they were never likely to agree with one another, they decided to finish their dispute by war, because they were, after all, people. And even though cities were razed to the ground and priceless treasures destroyed for ever and countless millions of people annihilated, at least the war came to an end and the question was finally decided.

And the professors and the wise men began to research and to publish their findings of how the world was flat because it was they, the flat-earthers, who had won the war.

And just in case there might be any different or dissenting opinion they collected all their enemies together, or those that were left of them, and they bundled them into cars and carriages and chariots. And then they drove the cars and the carriages and the chariots over the cliff at the edge of the world, because after all, they were right.

EARS

There was a soldier who fought in the great wars in defence of civilization and democracy who sent the ears of his dead enemies home to his friends.

They thought they were dried apricots because they were a bright yellow and orange colour.

They ate them.

They were, depend upon it, disgusted and horrified and more than even concerned when they learned the truth. This is because they were, after all, nice white people with a good clean liberal conscience.

That did not mean, however, that they did not enjoy them nor find them exceedingly delicious.

THE ONLY TRUE REASON WHY
CAIN KILLED HIS BROTHER ABEL

One evening when Abel was about to go out to a dance he came down the stairs. Cain was sitting at the table scratching his locks and generally minding his own business.

"What's up? Where are you going?" he asked, for the sake of saying something or anything at all.

"It's none of your fuckin' business," Abel said, trying to prevent his nose from taking off into the air. "Who the fuck are you you fuckin' fucker for askin' me where the fuck am I goin'. And as I'm at it why the fuck are you wearin' my fuckin' purple fuckin' polka-dot tie?"

"Because, it was lying in the heap on the floor through which you jump every morning. You missed it and I thought as you weren't wearing it it would be perhaps all right or even OK"

"Well it's not fuckin' OK and didn't I tell you not to lay a fuckin' hand on any fuckin' thing belongin' to me a-fuckin-gen?"

"Well, you did, of course, but so what and what is that to me? It's not as if you are going to do anything about it, is it, now?"

Cain reached for the big bread-knife on the kitchen table and without pausing to adjust his aim stuck it viciously into his brother's neck. He made sure that he would never wear his purple polka-dot tie again as he slashed it through the middle as he pulled the knife out of his throat. It was covered in blood anyway.

THE THIRD WORLD

There was a rich man and a poor man. The poor man had to carry the rich man around on his back. They went here, there, and everywhere. They went up hill and down dale. They met Tom, Dick and Harry and Rothschilds and Rockefellers and O'Reillys. The poor man slept in the cardboard city created by the rich and the rich man slept in the glitzy hotel built by the poor. But every morning the same sun shone on the rich man's face and on the poor man's bum.

The rich man dug his heels into the poor man's neck in order to feel more comfortable. The poor man wrapped the rich man's ankles around his chest in order to feel more safe.

Whenever they saw anything valuable or useful on their journey around the world – food or jewels or oil or riches or minerals or fish – the rich man would kindly ask, "Hey, why don't you pick that up and I will carry it for you?"

translated by the author